THIS HOLLOW HEART

SEASONS OF LEGEND BOOK ONE

NICKI CHAPELWAY

DRAGONFLIGHT PRESS

Cover by Maria Spada

Under the dust jacket art by Amira Naval

Map by Chaim Holtjer

Edited by Wisteria Editing

Proofed by Grace Morris

Formatted by Jes Drew

CONTENTS

To my best and only cousins Jason and Joshie.

K

THE SPICE ISLANDS

VATN OCEAN

RUSKU

SEA

· RUSKHAZAR ·

F RUINS

EINAN

ELLEF

SEA

N

Reglagrad

ERN   DESERTS

Chain 2021

CHAPTER ONE
NATASYA

Year 26 of the Third Era

I know what everyone thinks of me, and it quite simply isn't true.

They all think I'm the merchant's daughter with more money than I have sense and that I'm devoted to my fiancé. They say that I swept in like a summer storm and wrapped every young man in town around my finger, none more so than Brom the Bones, the descendant of Sunder Hollow's founder.

However, under the guise of the charming damsel, I'm hiding a far darker secret.

My father may have once been a merchant, but he can hardly be classified as just a *merchant* anymore—not when he runs a criminal empire. I am wealthy, but I also have a lot of sense. And I'm not devoted in the least to my fiancé. I just need what he can give me, an ancient spellbook that has been passed through his family.

I certainly didn't come in like a summer storm; I crept in like the darkness of an autumn night, wrapping my fingers around what isn't mine like the dark steals the light too early in the evening.

But I know my own story well enough, and I'm fine with misleading everyone. What I truly want to know is what *his* story is.

I watch almost spellbound as the hooded gentleman makes his way down the middle of the road, straight into the heart of town. Sunder Hollow does not get visitors, that is a well-known fact. It's why my coming here caused such a stir. The town is situated so far south that it can barely be considered a part of Ruskhazar and sits right at the foot of two impassable mountains.

Anyone with anywhere to be circumvents Sunder Hollow.

If our geographical isolation weren't enough, there's also the fact that the town is built only a stone's throw from a mass grave of sorcerers.

Many people in Ruskhazar are superstitious and fearful. Since there are those who can raise the dead, burial grounds are kept a good distance away from any towns for fear of the shambling undead striking against the living.

If there is one thing, they fear more than the possibility of the dead coming back, it's the sorcerers that can raise the dead.

So, it stands to reason that dead sorcerers are the most fearsome creatures in existence. And there are a hundred of them buried just past that hill and a short trek through the woods.

I fold my arms as the stranger draws to a stop. As if summoned by his presence, the whole town begins spilling into the streets. The smith stops working at his craft and old lady Margery stops hanging up her wash. Everyone watches the stranger as a hush fills the town.

It's quite a different response than what I received when I first arrived here a few months ago. At that time, I had been swarmed by a dozen would-be suitors wanting to make a good first impression, but I'd only had eyes for one man.

Brom the Bones, the unofficial leader of this town.

My eyes flick to him now as he strides forward, the gravel of the town road crunching under his boots. His thick dark hair is pulled back in a ponytail, revealing a striking jawline. Indeed, his features are all so strong and straight, looking almost as if they had been carved from stone like the statues in my father's lair hidden deep within the mountains. The only imperfection in his appearance is a nose that is just a little crooked from a time it was broken in the past.

He is truly quite a striking figure, and as a Lower Elf, he is also extremely tall and brawny. I could do worse for a fiancé, that much I know for sure. I know that my father was concerned about me marrying Brom all to get that spellbook. He married for love, and still adores my mother even today. I have to be careful when I walk in on them together, or I might just see something I don't want to.

He always told me and my sisters to marry for love, that the power would come later, but I'll admit that I don't have quite the same romantic notions as he does.

After all, I'm a necromancer. I would be hated by nearly anyone who learned about my unholy hobby of knitting together bones and sinew to make servants of the deceased. Repulsed more like.

My father may have found someone morally scrupulous enough to overlook his deeds, but I do not kid myself to believe that I will find the same.

For someone to love me, I must lie to them about an essential part of myself. And how could it truly be love if that is the case?

No, I will not be finding love, but I could do worse than Brom, and at least with him, I get a spellbook out of the deal. I also admit that I somewhat relish the irony of marrying into one of the most renowned magical bloodlines, that of a Magicker so powerful that he helped found the Academy of Magickers.

They say that since then no one has ever mastered magic quite like him and his fellow founders.

And I'm marrying his descendant. Me, a sorceress. Ah how Boris the Conjurer would roll in his grave if he knew... and I wouldn't even have to command his bones to cause him to do so.

"Ho, stranger," Brom calls raising his hand. "What is your name and business in this town?"

The stranger turns his head taking in the townsfolk gathered on either side of the street around him. Then he raises his gaze, he seems to pause when he sees me. Eyes hidden by his hood linger on me, and I shiver slightly before he finally turns to Brom. He reaches up, sweeping off his hood to reveal a head of chin length hair the color of tarnished gold.

A white streak running through his hair and slightly pointed ears reveal him to be of Higher Elf descent and the blue of his tunic peeking out from under his robe show that he is knowledgeable in the magical arts.

Or else a sorcerer like me who only wears the colors of magic to hide his true intentions.

His eyes, however, are what truly draw my attention. A strange and eerily pale blue, they seem to pierce straight to the soul as he turns that gaze back to me.

"You may call me Evengi," he says. "Evengi Ichabod, and my business here is my own."

CHAPTER TWO
NATASYA

"Last I checked, it isn't illegal for someone to enter a town," I murmur although I doubt that Brom has the presence of mind to listen to me. He's too preoccupied pacing in front of the fire fuming over the fact that someone would dare to step foot in his town and not show him the proper deference he deserves.

Despite my words, I find myself just as agitated as Brom by the newcomer's appearance. I'm just better at hiding it.

No one ever comes to Sunder Hollow with good intentions. I, of all people, should know that.

"Who does he think he is?" Brom growls out, still all fire and rage.

Who indeed?

I suppose I should just be glad that Brom wasn't like this when I arrived. I explained my presence about as well as this Evengi did, but fortunately I had other things working in my favor.

My father always said that my pretty face will get me far in this world.

No one expects the beautiful young woman to be the heretical sorceress. No, that sort of role is filled by old hags or perhaps by a Higher Elf like my sister Corallin since we made everything they did illegal, so now they are eternally branded as criminals.

But little old me?

Oh no, I'm not suspicious in the slightest. Not like our cloaked friend who entered town earlier today with his vague words and his superior attitude. His presence begs the question of what he is up to, and just why he decided to pay our sleepy little town a visit.

For perhaps the first time in our engagement I find myself fully agreeing with Brom. I want to know who this Evengi Ichabod is, and I want to know it now.

But how exactly do I go about getting this information? A simple and direct line of questioning has already proved ineffective. Evengi seems to have secrets that he is unwilling to part with.

So, I'll just have to convince him that he actually wants to part with them. To me, at least. And I have at least one great weapon in my arson, something that Brom lacks. I have guile.

"I know that you want more information, dear," I coo, twirling my fiery red hair around my finger.

Brom presses his mouth into a thin line. "I fear this bodes ill, Natasya. I have a grim feeling about this new-comer."

I cluck my tongue. "You only worry about what you don't understand. That's it, there's one thing for it," I state as I push to my feet, pushing back the seat of the desk I was perched at. "We must throw a party to honor Evengi, welcoming him to Sunder Hollow. With such an honor, surely, he will not refuse you when you ask for more information."

Brom's face softens as he smiles at me, but that smile quickly slips off his face as he turns toward the window. He rests a hand on my hip, drawing me closer. "There's something oddly familiar about him. Like I met him before, I just can't think of where."

This causes me to pause. I turn to Brom, arching my brow. "Where—" I begin, but then I pause and clear my throat, remembering to stick with my sweetened tone around him. "Where do you think you know him from?"

He shakes his head, his eyes getting a far-off look. "I can't quite place it, but I'm sure that I know him." He sighs, running a hand down his face. "I'm worried about what this might mean for Sunder Hollow."

I reach up, resting a hand on the side of his face and offer him a smile. "Whatever it is, we will face it together."

The words echo in my mind like an empty promise. It's true, I may be marrying Brom the Bones, but how can we truly do anything *together* when he doesn't even know who I am? And if he did, he would likely hate me for it.

I'll be there for him, his perfect little wife, and all the while he will never be what I need. All I want is someone to be my equal in mind and spirit, a man I don't have to lie to.

Brom is just too good a person to ever be that.

I turn away before Brom sees my face fall and start for the door.

"Where are you headed?" he asks.

I flash a quick smile at him over my shoulder. "If there's to be a ball tonight, then I think I'll go prepare."

Brom's face lights up. "I suppose I will just have to do the ball tonight then; any excuse to see you in a gown."

I laugh as I let myself out of the house. However, my smile doesn't stay in place as I cross the threshold. I grip my skirts as I try to imagine a whole life with Brom, pretending to be one thing within the walls of his house and then becoming something else entirely as soon as I step foot outside.

I sigh heavily, pressing the back of my head against the wooden door, but my musings are quickly interrupted by a new voice piercing through the silence of the foggy afternoon air.

"My, my, what's a pretty girl like you doing looking so sad?"

I straighten, opening my eyes to find myself staring into the startling blue gaze of none other than Evengi Ichabod.

CHAPTER THREE
NATASYA

"What are you doing here?" I blurt out before I can remember my manners and that this town knows me as something other than the crime lord's daughter who demands a certain amount of obedience from others.

Evengi pushes off from where he was leaning against the fence and skips over a small stream that runs through Brom's front yard. He drops into a half bow, a smirk written across his angular face. "A good day to you as well."

I clear my throat, taking a moment to compose myself. I reach up, running a hand through my hair and then trail it down my skirts. "Forgive my outburst," I say, dropping honey in my tone just as I have always done with Brom. It works to get him to do exactly what I want, maybe it will do the same with this Evengi. "It is only that you startled me."

Evengi clicks his tongue. "What would you have to be afraid of in such a... *quaint* town like this?"

He says quaint like it's an insult. When I first arrived here, I would have been inclined to agree. Sunder Hollow does not offer much in the form of recreation, but I have discovered that it offers me a lot in something that I have discovered to be quite invaluable. Seclusion.

I ignore his question and instead hold out my hand to him. "I don't believe we have been officially introduced. My name is Natasya Valadottir."

"Evengi Ichabod at your service, my lady." Evengi clasps my hand as he says this. His palm is smooth and his fingers uncalloused. So, he is not a craftsman or a warrior. Nor does he seem to have a writing bump or ink stains a scholar would carry.

Perhaps he is a minor lord, which would explain why Brom recognizes him. I don't know of any higher born lords of the name Ichabod, and I tend to make it a business to know things about people in power, but there are many lowborn lords who own small plots of ancestral land who are beneath my notice.

Or he could be a Magicker as his robes would suggest such, but just because he wears blue doesn't mean that he attended the Academy or studied the magical arts. I've come to learn that most Magickers are physically incapable of not blurting out that they are the Magicker the moment any conversation with them begins.

Evengi doesn't release my hand, instead he keeps it held up between us, his thumb moving absently as it traces a circle across my palm. I stifle a shudder that races unbidden up my spine.

"Your surname, it is Highlander?" he asks after a long moment.

"Yes, indeed," I reply, taking some comfort in being able to ease into the familiar conversation topic even though Evengi and his sudden appearance in Sunder Hollow has me feeling on edge and out of sorts. "My mother is a Highlander and my father a Lower Elf. My sisters and I were adopted by them, and I decided on taking a surname. I think that Valadottir has a bit more of a graceful ring to it than my father's name of The Eel."

As I speak, I find myself studying Evengi. He is taller than me and quite lean; his face is extremely angular with a jutting jaw and long straight nose. A white streak stands out in sharp contrast to his dirty golden hair, betraying some elven heritage. His eyes have a sort of ethereal glow to them, also speaking to Higher Elf blood flowing in his veins.

I am not quite sure just what it is about him, but I find his appearance almost spellbinding. Perhaps, it is the intelligence that flashes in those pale blue eyes, or the charm to his smirk as he says. "I have heard that each Lower Elf takes on his surname as a sort of title for what he has done. Pray, what did your father do to earn the surname *The Eel*?"

I blink taken slightly aback by his line of questioning. Many people just accept names for what they are, not seeking the deeper meaning within. Even Brom who is a Lower Elf did not ask me about my father's name.

"Why because he is a merchant," I manage to say as I recover from my surprise. "He was so slippery in getting away with the best bargain that he took on the name Eel."

At my words, a smile breaks across Evengi's face. He ducks his head as a slight chuckle escapes.

"You find this amusing?"

He drops my hand and raises his own to run through his hair. It rustles against the collar of his shirt as he looks me over. "No, no, I quite enjoy learning people's stories. Your father just happens to carry one of the more unique names I have ever heard. And to think that he willingly chose it for himself."

I fold my arms across my chest and arch my brow. "Says the man named Ichabod." His name claims he is without honor, but he would insult Eel?

His smile is back, but it is more forced. "I'm afraid I wasn't given the luxury of choosing my own surname."

He reaches up rubbing the back of his neck as he says this, and his eyes dart to the side so that they are no longer holding mine. I have picked up on many talents growing up in a den of thieves and assassins.

Being able to tell when someone is lying is one of those skills.

And Evengi is lying to me... about his name of all things?

"You never answered my earlier question," I say before the silence can go on for too long. Even as I speak, my mind is whirling with questions.

"About?" he asks as he slides his four fingers into a pocket in his pants.

"What are you doing here?"

"Well, after I got myself situated in the boarding house, I decided to take a stroll through and see the village. That stroll brought me to this doorstep and I thought I'd be friendly and say hi."

I notice that he only answers as to why he is *here* in Brom's front yard, not in Sunder Hollow as a whole.

"Well, I'm glad you're here," I reply with a smile.

This clearly surprises him. He moves back a step. "Oh?"

I think he knows exactly what I mean by *here,* and it isn't Brom's front yard. But since he refuses to acknowledge the larger scheme of things, so will I. If he will leave me guessing, then I won't give him the courtesy of being straightforward.

"Indeed, it saves me the trouble of tracking you down. We are holding a ball tonight in the village square. You are invited to come. Indeed, I must insist you come. After all, it will be thrown in your honor." I lean toward him, tucking my hands behind my back. "After all, it's so rare that we get visitors here in Sunder Hollow."

Evengi is not intimidated by my suddenly invading his space, like Brom would have been. He would have broken contact and moved away stammering something idiotic, but instead Evengi just leans toward me until there is hardly an inch of space between the two of us and whispers, "And yet, here we both are."

CHAPTER FOUR
EVENGI

T he spirits are restless here in Sunder Hollow, and I'm determined to figure out why.

I can hear them crying out, whispers of abominations and injustices. I stroll down the muddy streets of this town that I can only describe as *quaint.* At least that's if I am to listen to my mother's teaching and save my tongue from saying any insults.

Tis never polite to insult, even if it's deserved.

"And the polite will rule the world," I whisper smiling slightly at my mother's adage. Oh, but she is a particular woman and far too prim for any of our gods. It's been too long since I've last visited my family. I will have to remedy that soon as I can, but first the ghosts.

Sunder Hollow may have some things going for it—things I have yet to witness—but its size is not one of them. The population is small, and the people mistrusting. I suppose I cannot blame them, in a town this small and isolated, these people are at risk of a large band of bandits raiding them or something far worse...

There are always the sorcerers who engage in their cultish practices. Many sorcerers choose to live in isolated areas where they can perform their heresies without the threat of a discovery. These are dangerous times, you come across the wrong mill and wind up as a human sacrifice.

Sacrifice, sacrifice, sacrifice... the spirits hiss and I find myself frowning. These spirits are more than restless. They are angry.

I wish that one would materialize in front of me so that I can speak to it, ask it important questions such as who killed it and how long it has been dead.

Spirits don't have a way of marking the passage of time, and so old wounds still drive them even if the person they wish to avenge may be long dead.

I twist my head, as cold air washes over me. To the people around me it may seem like just the wind, but I know better. It's the frustrated breath of the spirits.

People go through their lives so blissfully ignorant, not realizing just how many of the spirits have lost their way and now exist somewhere between the world of the living and Skyhold, the realm of the gods and the dead.

They trust that upon their death, Thyre, the head god and guardian of the afterlife, will collect their souls and bring them to him. But those who have died in especially violent ways often remain behind, bound to this world by the nature of their death. And they aren't the only ones to become trapped spirits.

Those seeking vengeance also lose their way.

Those who are still too connected to Ruskhazar and do not wish to leave.

Heretics.

There are far more ghosts here than anyone would realize. It's just that most people cannot see them since the ghosts spend most of their time in noncorporeal forms, only taking on visible attributes in extremely rare circumstances.

The rest of the world can't see what I can see.

Keavor says that it's because of my accident during my first year at the academy. I had been stupid and not taken the proper precautions in the Spellcraft, and a spell backfired on me. The spell would have killed me, perhaps it did, but the academy healers were on hand and were able to revive me. Ever since then I have been able to hear the spirits.

I was a part of the spirit world for a few precious seconds. When I touched it, no matter how briefly, it left its mark on me. And I on it.

I suppose I should be glad that the accident happened because it's given me my purpose.

I'm not sure what I would be if I weren't a ghost hunter.

And Sunder Hollow has to be one of the most haunted towns I've ever come across.

CHAPTER FIVE
NATASYA

G rowing up as a reclusive assassin lord's daughter meant that I did not get out much. In truth, I spent a great deal of time in my mother's inn where it was deemed "safe" and "appropriate" for a girl of my age to be.

While my sister Corallin meted out assassination contracts, I had to sit up in the rafters listening to mother's bard practice his songs for hours on end. While my twin Bronwyn busied herself with her closest companions—her books—I was bored to death.

Father had his acquaintances from his respectable businesses though, and eventually I caused enough trouble at the inn by pulling tiny pranks with my sorcery that father relented and brought me along with him on those meetings. Those were tedious, of course, but occasionally something would come up, and he would have to attend to business in the world of shadows while I was around.

It was at one such meeting that I met Taryn.

Her father Michael was a vampire lord and her mother Bryn was a disgraced member of the Kotov line. The Kotovs are a powerful noble family with a pedigree in magic that stretches back to before the academy was founded, but that wasn't why my father was interested in Bryn and her husband. After all, she had been disowned.

No, it was because Bryn was the sister of Creed Kotov, a man who is arguably the most powerful necromancer of this current age.

And as such, he is near impossible to locate. But Elwis kept tabs on Creed through Bryn and Michael.

When I met Taryn, we immediately became close friends, as close as sisters really. After much begging, my father relented and let me spend my summers at Taryn's family home with the promise that I would study diligently during the winter months and share any necromancy secrets I might learn from Creed's family—even if they Taryn and her immediate family were actually all magickers.

It was during my time with Taryn's family that I was able to enjoy the occasional ball. Due to the vampirism, Taryn's father was extremely reclusive, but always tried to keep up good relations with the neighboring lords. So, when his family was invited to a ball, they would attend. If I was staying there, I was able to tag along and pretend that I had been born into nobility instead of as the abused daughter of a drunk farmer who got lucky when an assassin decided to take pity on her.

I'm sure that the ball Brom will be holding in Evengi's honor here in Sunder Hollow will not be anywhere near as enchanting as the balls I attended alongside Taryn and her family, but I'm still excited.

I've always loved an excuse to put on a pretty dress and put on airs.

I pull a pink dress with billowing skirts from my wardrobe and hold it up to my chest as I sway in front of my looking glass before I pull it on. Father bought a lovely little house in Sunder Hollow for me to use while I work toward getting that spellbook. It's the second nicest home in town, and fortunately, came up for sale only a few months before we arrived here when the previous owner died in a tragic "*accident*".

The dress was a gift from Taryn herself. She gave it to me on my nineteenth birthday, but I haven't had much opportunity to wear it before now.

I smile at my reflection. This dress makes me look just like a noble woman. Standing here, in a house that my father bought me. The second largest in town, but one of the smallest of the houses my father owns, and it reminds me of just how far I've come.

I'm not that dirty faced urchin who dug up roots to try to eat them and spent my days hiding from my father and twin alike. No, I'm a lady now. A pretty one at that, but more importantly I'm powerful.

No one will ever push me around and tell me what to do again.

There's a creak as the cellar door opens, and I turn just as the skeleton shambles in. "What do you think, Father?" I ask with a smile into the empty sockets of the skeleton. But there is no reply from the knitted together bones.

Even though he is my father, nothing but the bones remain. A hollow husk of the man who sired me with no eyes to see or tongue to speak and no heart to finally give his daughter love.

I wish that when you reanimate a body, you can bring back their soul. What I would give to be able to raise my father's bones and show him the daughter he was so ashamed of that he drank himself in a stupor. The girl that he not only beat but encouraged her sister to beat.

According to him, we both killed our mother when she birthed us. But I came out last, I delivered the final blow.

"One daughter she could have managed, why did you have to be there?" was what he always said.

"So that I can become ten times what you will ever be," I whisper as I step toward the skeleton. I trace a finger across one of the bones that make up his shoulder. Even after all these years of practicing necromancy, he is my favorite to reanimate.

It isn't all for spite. I'm also sentimental, and whether either of us wanted it or not, he was my father.

If he wouldn't care for me in life, then he will in death.

"Will you help me do the clasps of my dress, Papa?" I ask my father's skeleton, even though no verbal command is actually required. Sorcery is not like magic in that it needs to be spoken; instead, sorcery is controlled by a mere thought.

It's so much more powerful than any magic, but perhaps that is why it is illegal. Because people fear the sort of power it grants.

Boney fingers start on my clasp as I turn my attention back to getting ready for the ball. Taryn picked the best dress for me. So many colors clash with my red hair and make it difficult to wear, but this pale pink instead compliments and brings out my coloring in a manner that I would not have expected.

The sleeves flare at my elbow and the skirts swoosh over my petticoats. I rest my hand over my heart and determine to thank Taryn the next time I see her for doing her part in making me the prettiest girl who will be in Sunder Hollow tonight.

I wonder if I should invite her to my wedding. On one hand, I would want her to be there, but on the other I worry that she will see right through me and know that I don't love my groom. For years, we lamented the fact that neither of us has brothers that the other can marry. The closest we came to being related is that at one point in time, there was an arrangement for her cousin to marry my cousin, but that fell through. Still, it doesn't matter. I've since realized that I don't need to be related by blood for us to be sisters.

After all, I don't share a drop of blood with Corallin or the rest of my adopted family. And yet they are just as much my family as my own twin Bronwyn.

Taryn is a sister of my soul, and I feel her with me as I wear this dress tonight.

"I think I'm ready," I tell myself, my looking glass, and the knitted bones behind me.

My father shambles back down to my cellar where I keep him hidden, and I put on the brightest smile I have, ready to enter that night and become someone else.

Someone that I might actually enjoy being.

CHAPTER SIX
NATASYA

I t's a crisp autumn night as I go out to the village square. The housewives of Sunder Hollow have been busy preparing for the impromptu ball, and the square is lit with candles that have been placed in carved out pumpkins to protect the flames from the occasional sharp, chill breeze.

While I was dressing with the aid of my skeleton butler, the townspeople decided it was time to show Evengi Ichabod that while we are a small town, we know how to throw a ball.

"My dear," Brom whispers in my ear as he comes up behind me. He takes my arm and guides it into the crook of his arm. "You look exquisite tonight."

I smile to myself, I do. And that's all Brom needs me to be, his pretty little bride-to-be to hang off his arm. There's no reason for him to ever need to know about the skeletons in my cellar because all we will ever be to each other is a trophy. And that's fine with me.

It would get too messy if there were true feelings involved. I mean, just look at Bronwyn. Wilder has the power to completely control her emotions and can either ruin her day or make it with a simple string of words. I can't imagine actually giving someone that sort of power over me.

"There's our gangly guest," I whisper to Brom, nodding my chin to Evengi who has stepped into the square. He's traded out his dusty traveling clothes for a fresh tunic of royal blue, a short purple cape hangs from his shoulders. His golden hair catches in the candlelight as he turns as if he realizes that we are talking about him.

I feel my breath clog in my throat as it seems almost as if his eyes lock on mine even across the distance of the village square. Evengi smiles to himself and begins to stride across the square toward us.

"I swear, Natasya, there is something about this Mr. Ichabod that is oddly familiar," Brom says to me.

I turn to him, my eyes flicking over my fiancé's features registering the concern he feels. I don't know who this

Evengi is, but his presence here could very well jeopardize me. I want Brom complacent, not worried and on edge.

Still, maybe if he is so focused on Evengi, he won't bother looking at me.

Fiddle and flute music fills the air, and the square begins to fill as the inhabitants of Sunder Hollow begin to party. We don't have a proper bard, but some men here have picked up some musical knowledge from the odd traveling minstrel who would stop and stay in the town. It's not any sort of traditional sounding music that I've heard in the outside world.

That music is lilting and subtle, this is rustic and haunting.

I plaster a smile on my face as Evengi strides toward us, a glass of spiced apple cider in his hand. "I appreciate this ball, Brom," he says, smacking Brom's arm with a sort of familiarity that causes my fiancé to frown.

"It was our pleasure," I say quickly before Evengi notices Brom's frustration. I'll admit, I find myself rather curious about this newcomer and why Brom finds him so familiar. I tell myself that it's simply because I need to protect my investment. A threat to Brom is a threat against my chances of getting that spellbook. I wrap my arm around Brom's waist, resting my hand on the spellbook resting there, reminding myself of what I'm doing this all for.

Brom mistakes my caress and pulls me closer, placing a kiss to the top of my head.

Evengi's eyes, too sharp, too cunning, dart to my hand, then to Brom, before finally landing on me. I stiffen slightly. He has no reason to suspect me of anything, and yet, I can't help but feel as though he takes in more than he should.

"I hope that you enjoy the evening. After all, you are the guest of honor," I say, hoping my tone doesn't betray how tense I feel.

Evengi smiles slowly as he holds out his hand palm up. "As the guest of honor, I suppose it's only fitting I use my auspicious title to claim a dance with the prettiest woman here."

I pull back slightly with surprise as Brom stiffens this time. Evengi Ichabod thinks I'm the prettiest woman here? Sunder Hollow may not be large, but there are a number of pretty lasses here who I catch standing huddled together staring at Evengi with admiration.

He could have his pick of any woman here; he is handsome and novel enough that if he proposed marriage, he would have a wife before the night is through.

Why would he go for the engaged woman here?

I can't help but feel flattered. Am I really so beautiful that Evengi would go for a hapless cause over someone readily available?

"Assuming it's fine with your betrothed, of course," Evengi adds after a moment, and I realize that I have left him standing there with his hand outstretched just a moment too long.

Brom laughs, but there is no humor in the sound. "Of course, just know I'll want her back before the evening is through."

I place my hand in Evengi's before I have the chance to consider my eagerness to do so. I tell myself that I'm just caught up in the beguiling mystery of Evengi Ichabod. That is why my heart races as I look up at him, the exhilaration of figuring out a puzzle. Just because that puzzle happens to be tall and handsome has nothing to do with it.

I glance over my shoulder at Brom as I move away. His jaw ticks as he watches us, and I can't help but feel a little good about that. It's nice to know that I'm desired.

Evengi pulls me into a dancing position and begins moving me through the steps, however, as he dances, I notice that he keeps his eyes on Brom who is watching us with his arms crossed. "You and your fiancé seem like quite the couple."

"I'm the woman of Brom's dreams," I say with a small laugh repeating the corny line he used on me when he first proposed. I can't help but smile slightly at the memory. If there is one thing that I can be assured of, it's that at least life with Brom will be quite amusing.

"Do you love him?" Evengi asks as he sweeps me under his arm. My skirts fan out around my legs as I twirl. I blame them for why I stumble.

"Love?"

He arches his brow as he steadies me. "You know, butterflies in your stomach, falling asleep with his name on your lips, the desire to start a family with him? That feeling."

I bite my lip as I look up into Evengi's eyes. He stares down at me awaiting an answer, and I silently curse myself for not immediately replying with an affirmative. It wouldn't be the first lie I've ever told. It certainly wouldn't even be the most egregious.

I pull my eyes away as I step to the side. Evengi follows making it look like just a part of the dance. "What does it matter to you?" I ask before I wince. Why can I not just say *yes*? I am only opening myself up for more questions from Evengi.

I never should have agreed to this dance. If I'd known it would turn into an inquisition, I would have remained safely by Brom's side. At least, he takes me at face value and knows better than to ask me ridiculous questions such as whether or not I love him.

So, what if I am trapped in a loveless engagement? Love is not something I lack nor is it something I need.

I have my father's love, my mother, my sisters. I have more love in my life than is entirely necessary.

"I am trying to figure out who you are is all," Evengi says simply like it's not the single most terrifying sentence I have ever heard.

The last thing I need is someone trying to figure me out. "Whatever for?" I ask as I paste a smile onto my face with great difficulty. As soon as the words are out of my mouth, I realize that I should have just laughed it all off and said something insipid such as "there isn't anything to figure out," or that I'm an "open book."

Evengi studies me. "Let's just say that I have a vested interest in Brom and leave it at that."

He drops me into a dip, and I gasp as my heart lurches into my chest. "You can't just say something so cryptic and leave it at that."

Evengi smirks. "I just did."

I open my mouth to protest but just then he leads me into another twirl. I'm dizzy as I am swung back around, finding my chest pressed against Evengi's hard one. I gasp for air as I look up at him. "Where did you learn to dance like that?"

"I'll tell you," he says gripping my waist and tugging me closer as he hooks his foot behind my ankle and takes off dancing across pavilion. We're moving so fast that it's like we're flying, and it takes every bit of what I learned about dancing while staying with Taryn to even manage to keep up. I have no chance to talk as we move back and forth and up and down the village square, as if we are one. I don't know where my foot ends or Evengi's leg begins. All I know is his guiding hands around my waist, gently but firmly holding me steady despite feeling as if his arms on me is the only thing keeping me from lifting into the air.

Suddenly, Evengi puts out his leg, draping me over it in a graceful dip. The sudden stop jolting me after the blur of motion. My skirts flare out around us both, creating a false sense of isolation. Like for a second, it's just him and me here instead of a village full of people watching us dance.

He stares at me for a long moment the both of us gasping for breath before he slowly straightens, pulling me up with him. He loosens his hold on me, but I notice that he doesn't entirely let go. His eyes sparkle offset by his flushed cheeks as he says. "But only if you tell me what you want with Brom the Bones."

I stare at him unsure how to describe the way this stranger makes me feel. He makes me feel almost how I always imagined the dead things I play with do. Marinette's on invisible strings, hanging to his every word and yet disgusted by it.

If I know what's good for me, I should make this Evengi my pretty little dead thing. He would ask far fewer questions when he is no longer a member of the living. It's what my father would expect from me.

Instead, I find myself smiling as I step away. "Why wouldn't I want to marry the handsomest man in town?"

Evengi's eyebrows shoot up, and I laugh slightly to myself as I turn only to find myself staring into the stony face of Brom the Bones. However, his attention isn't on me at all, but on Evengi. "Mind if I cut in?" he asks, but from the tone of his voice it's clear it isn't a request.

"Of course," Evengi says graciously as he places my hand into Brom's. "I thank you for sharing her." Then to me he winks. "I'll keep my end of the bargain whenever you decide to be straight with me. We can discuss my dancing later."

Then he walks off, leaving me standing next to Brom while he squeezes my hand just a little too hard. The both of us staring after Evengi Ichabod and wondering just who this traveler who came to our small town might be.

CHAPTER SEVEN

EVENGI

I shouldn't have made such a scene, but I can't find it in myself to regret that decision.

That dance was the most fun I've had in a long time. It has been a while since I've had a worthy partner.

I raise the glass to my lips and take a sip of the tart apple cider within, wishing all the while that the ghosts would be quiet so I can properly think. Or better yet, they would actually say something that might just help me to figure out what's going on here. But their murmurs and hisses remain incoherent, just a buzz of noise in my ear.

There are always ghosts around but never so many. Nor are they usually so loud and angry. This is a telltale sign of necromancy or some other desecration of the dead is happening. Given the history of this town the question is if I'm dealing with a living necromancer... or if this is still an aftershock of the battle that took place at the mass grave this town is built next to.

One hundred necromancers is an impressive number, so even if it happened five hundred years ago, I wouldn't be surprised if they still have the ability to affect the spirits today.

But then again this is more than an echo. It's almost as if the souls have been stirred up. The past battle might explain their numbers, but it doesn't explain why they are so instigated. They were always here but something newly got their attention and got them riled up like this. Which brings me back to my theory that there's a necromancer here. A living and actively practicing necromancer.

It makes sense that they would come here, this must be hallowed ground to them, a place full of so many remains of their own kind. If there's two things that necromancers love, it's dead things and a sense of superiority over their fellow necromancers.

They all want to be the best necromancer there ever was as if there's some sort of art to playing puppet master to dead things. And to display that power over other necromancers by reanimating the corpses of their rivals? It's perhaps a necromancer's favorite thing to do.

So no, I'm quite certain there's a necromancer here, and I need to find them and make them face the justice of the gods if I intend to get a moment's peace from these infernally loud ghosts.

I twitch my head slightly, a habit that I'd thought I'd broken but then I twitch my head again, my neck moving of its own accord as if I'm trying to shake the sound out of my ear.

I grimace as I look up to see Natasya watching me from where she is standing next to her fiancé Brom. I raise my glass slightly and smirk.

She rolls her eyes and looks away, but I catch her continue to watch me out of the corner of her eye. It seems as though I've managed to bewitch Brom's pretty little fiancée at least half as much as she has bewitched me.

I feel a slight pang of guilt when I remember that Brom is my friend, even though it was long ago, and he likely doesn't remember it. But I quickly assuage it when I remember that the only reason, I am interested in Natasya is that I'm suspicious of her. I don't know just what I suspect her of, perhaps she is even my necromancer, but one thing I know for certain is that she is not who she appears to be.

I know a false premise when I see one. After all, my life has been one false premise or the other since I became a ghost hunter.

I'm doing him a favor if I get her attention off of him. At best, she's just after his title and worst-case scenario, she is looking for a sacrifice for some dark ritual.

Either way, if I can draw her attention away from him then I can save my former friend some heartache and agony when he realizes that his lovely fiancée is not quite the woman she has led him to believe she is.

I glance around, taking in the people of Sunder Hollow. There's a small group of ladies who seem to keep edging nearer, looking at me as if they are contemplating devouring my soul or something. I stifle a shiver and glance to my right. I find a portly older woman standing off to the side clapping her hands along with the tune.

She seems a bit bored and looks the type to gossip so I step toward her. I clear my throat. "Care to dance?"

Her face breaks out in a wide grin, one that I cannot help but return. It seems that, despite my duplicitous nature and borderline betrayal of an old friend, I have still managed to make someone's night. Now I can only hope that she can help make mine by shedding some light on certain areas I'm having a hard time understanding.

"My name is Evengi," I say as I pull her into a dance position and begin moving to time with the fiddle players.

"Oh, I know who you are," she says smiling up at me. I believe that she intends to sound coy, but her response is just a bit unsettling.

"You seem like the type of woman who is well informed," I say smoothly, determined to not allow the conversation to get derailed. I was not as successful as I would have liked with Natasya, and I intend to not make the same mistake twice.

"Indeed," she replies with a titter. "I can tell you anything you want to know about Sunder Hollow. Why, I've lived here my whole life and known most everyone here for just as long."

I smile down at her. "That must be nice."

I've traveled across all the land of Ruskhazar, seen so many people that their faces have begun to blur, witnessed so many sights that it all becomes the same. Once I would have scoffed at the narrow view of an individual who has never left their small town, but now I just feel weary. I can never have the experience she described. That sort of familiarity sounds appealing after so many years spent on the road, hopping from one inn to the next and never knowing where I'll lay my head for the night.

I've spent so long away from home that it doesn't feel like mine anymore.

Sometimes, I feel like a leaf blowing in the wind. I haven't the control of where I'll end up, all I know is that I don't belong with the oak I fell from.

"And you feel safe in Sunder Hollow?" I ask as I move us in a circle.

She rolls her eyes, waving away my words. "Oh, it's just superstition that makes people think that old graveyard is trouble. No necromancers come here, not with Brom the Bones as our leader, he carries his ancestor's legacy."

"You speak of Brom with great admiration."

"I've heard mighty awful things said about Lower Elves, how they see themselves better than the rest of us, but the Bones has never put on airs he didn't deserve. And while he is aloof sure, I've never gotten the impression that he believed himself better than us. Indeed, the girls here, myself included, were all so disappointed he decided to marry that merchant's daughter from out of town instead of one of us. That disappointment didn't last long though because then you arrived." The woman leans forward, resting her head against my chest. I quickly turn her in a spin to move her away.

I glance over in the direction of Brom, but he is no longer watching me, seemingly appeased now that I'm dancing with someone other than his fiancée. Natasya, however, is staring at me with such intensity that it feels as though she is trying to bore her gaze into me.

"So, you don't approve of his fiancée?" I ask as I bring the woman back around.

She presses her lips together, clearly not relishing my asking about Natasya. "I'm sure she's a nice enough girl. Heard her father is filthy rich too, a powerful landowner as well as a merchant, but she could have had her pick of any man in Ruskhazar. Why would she come here for Brom? I think she is title hunting. It's the one thing her father dearest couldn't provide her with."

I feel my eyebrows raise. There would be many lords in Reglagrad willing to throw their titles her way just to get a smile from a girl as pretty as that. I should know, before I became a ghost hunter, I would have been the first in that line.

Natasya is beautiful and young lords lack ambition and the purpose I found in my service to the goddess Neltruna. She could have had her pick, easily. Especially if she is as rich as this woman claims, many of the older nobility are not as wealthy as they would like, especially with the businessmen with the newer money that keep popping up.

She didn't need to come all the way out to Sunder Hollow if all she wanted was a title.

No, this woman is right to ask it... why Brom?

CHAPTER EIGHT
NATASYA

D espite its exciting start, the rest of the evening is quite dull. Brom, in his jealousy won't let me leave his side, so I have to stand here and listen to him discuss how pumpkin and corn harvest is going and arranging trade avenues with the farmers who grow crops for him.

All the while, I am forced to watch the women of Sunder Hollow fawn over Evengi like they are a murder of crows and he's a shiny new trinket they all want to claim for their own.

I narrow my eyes as one of the women, a pretty golden-haired lass who once told me that she and Brom were the closest of friends even though he has never mentioned her, caresses Evengi's arm.

"How in Skyhold has he managed to charm all of Sunder Hollow?" Brom asks, and I startle realizing that he has ended his conversation and has now followed my gaze. "He isn't even that handsome, and I certainly have yet to hear him say a single intelligent thing."

I reach out, patting his arm. "No one is saying that he should take your place as the lord of this village."

He harrumphs. Brom has many qualities, but modesty isn't one of them. He would never be able to share his position as the greatest and best and most admired of Sunder Hollow.

He steps forward, resting his foot on a bale of hay. "Gather close, my good people. I have a ghost story to tell," Brom says, commanding the people of Sunder Hollow just as I've seen him do on many occasions. They all seem to hang off his words.

I take this as an opportunity to finally break away from his side. I move through the crowd that gathers around Brom ready to hear the tale. I sidle up next to Evengi, bumping the pretty little golden-haired girl with my hip. "You simply must hear Brom spin a tale, he has such a way about it."

Evengi glances at me raising his eyebrow. "Oh, really?"

"Yes, even though most stories he tells are already folk tales that everyone here knows, he tells it in such a way that it makes it seem almost new."

"That's quite a talent," Evengi says. "It's a pity that being a bard doesn't pay as well as being a lord. Your fiancé may have missed his calling."

I titter a small laugh as the golden-haired girl throws me a dark look, and Brom begins his story.

"As we all know, many years ago there was a battle. The battle was waged in Sunder Hollow, but it was for the future of all Ruskhazar."

Brom unhooks his spellbook and opens it. His mouth moves as he silently utters a spell from within. A dark mist forms in front of him, taking on the shapes of men.

As Brom speaks he waves his arm out. "The enemy numbers were great indeed, a hundred necromancers terrible and able, and on the side of good there was but one. However, this was no mere warrior. The lone bastion against this evil was Borus the Conjurer, one of four founders of the Academy of Magickers, and he was not going to allow the evil to win without a fight. Not on that night."

I fold my arms feeling a tiny stab of ire at Brom's description of necromancy. I know that his whole family legacy is built off that defeat of those necromancers, but it still wounds me that my future husband will never be able to accept that part of me.

There are precious few in Ruskhazar who would. My father was fortunate indeed to find my mother, a woman who would love him as he is—necromancy and all. Of course, she was a smuggler, so she was already well acquainted with the shadowy underbelly of Ruskhazar.

It's like they were a match made in Skyhold.

And Bronwyn found a vampire who could not find acceptance anywhere else.

But I doubt the gods would make a match for the likes of me. After all, at the end of the day I'm just a girl who desecrates her father's bones. That's the kind of thing that the gods detest.

Evengi glances at me out of the corner of his eye, and I quickly relax my stance. I don't know what it is about Evengi, but his eyes seem to take in more than I'd want anyone to notice. Not with me living a duplicitous life here.

The images begin fighting one lone figure, this one is represented by a glowing mist, as Brom goes on to describe the battle in great detail. I know the story well, Borus created more magical constructs than any magicker has been able to create before or since. With nothing but his faith in Meruna and his spellbook, he made a whole army out of magic and with it defeated the army of necromancers. It's why I'm so set on getting my hands on that spellbook.

That spellbook is capable of defeating an army of necromancers in the right hands.

Even in the wrong hands it is powerful. If someone as ill versed in magic as Brom can use this spellbook to create a story out of the air, then there's no knowing what sort of powers this spellbook would hold in the hands of someone who would actually be able to use it.

My sister Bronwyn is the designated magicker in the family, and I know for a fact that she would dedicate the better part of eternity to unraveling every spell within until she knows them better than the man who wrote them. And finally, that spellbook can be used for more than just cheap parlor tricks.

It can be used to further my father's empire.

With the power scrawled out on those pages, my father will consolidate his role as the most powerful man in all of Ruskhazar.

"Borus buried the bodies of those necromancers in Heretic's Rest and then went on to build Sunder Hollow at the site of his greatest victory," Brom says. "But one should always be wary where necromancers are involved. Living or dead."

Brom smiles as the mist takes on the form of a burial mound which a hand shoots out of it. Someone in the crowd gasps. "It was once said that the end of the world will come with the rising of the dead. Some would even say that the end has already begun, but I say that can't be. Because when that end comes, we here at Sunder Hollow will be the first to know." Brom leans over the crowd grinning darkly. "Because we will be the first to fall to the vengeance of the necromancers. You can feel it in the Autumn wind, the fury of the spirits of Sunder Hollow who hate all the living and wish to make us become like them."

Brom snaps the book shut and the mist dissolves to the sound of applause. Brom looks at the crowd grinning fondly his ill-humor displaced.

"What a macabre tale," Evengi says with a little shudder.

"It's just a story." I laugh lightly. "Don't tell me that you're scared of ghosts, Mr. Ichabod."

"Aren't you?" he asks arching his brow. "They are not harmless."

I let out a titter that I perfected while Brom was courting me. "The fact that you believe in them at all!"

"There are too many witnesses of hauntings for me to ever discredit the existence of ghosts." Evengi tilts his head as he steps away. "Oh, I can assure you that ghosts are very much real, and the dead do rise. And the end of the world? It began at the dawn of the third era."

CHAPTER NINE
NATASYA

The forest is still and quiet. A welcome relief from the
hubbub of the party that went on for far too long.
We are now in the wee hours of the morning, and I have
very little time for myself before I must once again become
Brom's doting fiancé.

I exhale loudly through my mouth, tilting my head back
as I listen to the dry rustle of the leaves as the nightly breeze
washes over them.

By now, after the months I've spent here, my feet know
the direction to take all on their own as I make it to the
clearing. The rest of the forest is immensely dense, but it's
almost as if not even the trees would choose to grow here.
Sitting at the center of the clearing is a large stone, cut into
the earth and engraved with ancient runic symbols.

Runes are known as the symbol of magic, but long ago it seems that even sorcerers used them. I dare not create a rune of my own for fear of being cursed by madness or perhaps just killed for my hubris.

I may be used to bending the rules as a sorcerer, but that is one rule I will never bend. The cardinal law of nature. Mortals are not meant to embrace the power of both magic and sorcery, they are two separate entities and the two are never supposed to meet.

So, I could never recreate this runic circle, but I still like to use it.

I move to the center. Suddenly, I feel my veins go abuzz with the power. I kneel down closing my eyes, sensing a pair of squirrel bones not far away. Typically, I must see the dead to control them, but in the center of this circle, it is as if I can feel them. Like they are an extension of myself.

I twist my fingers calling the squirrels bones to rise. I hear it rustle to my right and send it in a circle scampering around. I laugh lightly at its antics.

People believe that necromancy is a desecration, but I prefer to see it as a second chance. For just this moment, this squirrel exists again.

How could something like that be wrong?

I tilt my finger towards me, summoning the squirrel as I look up. I freeze when I see a figure step out of the woods.

I'm on my feet in a second as the moon comes out from a set of clouds, revealing Evengi Ichabod standing there, still dressed in the tunic he wore during the party.

"Natasya?" he asks as if I'm the one who shouldn't be here. As if this isn't my sanctuary. He tilts his head. "What are you doing here?"

My eyes dart down to the skeleton squirrel sitting by the root of a tree staring at me from its empty eye sockets. I quickly wave my hand deconstructing its bones. Evengi turns, realizing that I'm looking at something over his shoulder. "What?"

I jerk my fingers, commanding the nearby leaves to drift over the bones. I hope that it looks as though they were blown there by the wind. I tuck my hands behind my back and smile over at Evengi. "This is my thinking spot," I say as sweetly as I can manage. Although, inwardly, I'm seething. How dare Evengi be here interrupting my time.

How dare he interrupt my life at all.

This man has only been in Sunder Hollow for a day and already he has done more to disrupt my ruse than anyone else here. He leaves me wondering if my carefully laid plans are quite as carefully laid as I had originally thought.

"Here?" he asks with a frown. "I studied at the academy for a while and I hate to tell you this, but I'm quite certain that this place was used for a dark ritual in the past."

"Whatever makes you say that?" I ask even though it's fairly obvious it was. It's why I like it here.

He winces as he jerks his head to the side, rubbing it against his shoulder, twice before he stiffens. He clears his throat. "Well, the circle you are standing on is one reason why I'd assume as much."

I pull up my skirts and gasp as if I'm looking down at them for the first time. "But I thought that runes were a form of magic."

"Runes are the written form of magic and not as predictable as the spoken form of it. Indeed, many non-magic wielders can use runes for the magic since the power is actually contained within the word itself and not in the caster." He steps forward, the leaves rustling as he moves. "And these runes speak of a dark magic indeed."

"They do?"

"I studied at the academy, remember. I learned to read the written form of magic." His eyes flick over it. "Soul magic, dead magic, killing magic," he looks up. "These are terrible runes."

"Oh," I say with a tittering laugh as if I don't already know that. I jump out of the circle, glancing back at it. "I guess I'll have to get a new thinking spot then."

"That might be prudent," Evengi says slowly, but there's something about his tone that makes me wonder if he actually believes my clueless act. Am I not convincing enough? No one in Sunder Hollow ever seemed to think so, but then in waltz Evengi. It's like he is toying with me, telling me things that he suspects I already know and letting me play a part.

No, I need to stop overthinking. I'm letting Evengi get in my head. No one has ever seen through my lies before. People see what they expect to see, and they don't expect to find a necromancer living in their midst.

Necromancers are monsters, violent, and reprehensible individuals...or so people believe. No one would expect to find one living peacefully next door. They would never expect a necromancer to not be performing any dark rituals and only reanimating dead squirrels to see them dance.

I pull my lip through my teeth. "What are you doing here, exactly?"

"Same as you, I suppose. I needed a moment of solitude." He arches his brow as if daring me to confront him and his paper-thin explanation, knowing full well that my explanation is no better. Either I take him at face value, or he will not take me at face value.

Oh, this man is toying with me indeed.

He holds out his arm to me. "But now that I've run into you, I'm honor bound to make certain that you get home safely. These woods are not safe. There are ghosts about."

"There you are with those ghosts again, Mr. Ichabod," I say as I slide my arm through the crook of his. At least if he is taking me away then he will have no opportunity to find that squirrel skeleton.

"I like to consider myself a personal expert on ghosts," he replies unphased as he begins walking. Straight toward the squirrel remains.

I try my best not to sound nervous as I keep talking. Anything to distract him. "Why couldn't you have found a normal area of expertise, like wildlife?"

"Now where would be the fun in that?" Evengi puts his foot down and I hear a crack. I wince as he lifts his foot. Through the unsettled leaves, I can see a glimpse of the pale bones. "What the Skyhold," he breathes as he bends down. I stand there paralyzed, unsure what to do to keep him from seeing those bones. I have only seconds to react, and I'm not proud of what my first inclination is.

I grab Evengi by the collar of his tunic, jerking him upright. His eyes widen and his mouth opens in question, but I don't let him get it out. Instead, I reach out tracing against his jawline. "I think I know the real reason you're out here tonight."

His eye darts to my finger then to me, the squirrel remains hopefully forgotten. "And wh—what would that be?" he stutters, sounding nervous. Ironic that he's alone in the woods with a necromancer, but the reason he is nervous is because a woman touched his face.

It makes me want to stroke his face again.

"The same reason I am," I whisper. "You were hoping to come across me so we could finish that last step of our dance."

Evengi's eyebrows furrow. "Our... dance?"

"Yes," I breathe, leaning closer. Evengi leans against the tree, tripping a bit over the root and fully leaving the squirrel remains behind. He presses his back against the tree even as I press myself against him. "Such a dance is incomplete without one final move."

Evengi licks his lips nervously. "I'm not sure I understand what you're talking about, and I like to consider myself an exceptional dancer."

"It's this," I breathe leaning forward and pressing my lips against his. It's supposed to be a brief kiss, one that gets his mind completely off the squirrel, but as I kiss him, I find myself apparently very desperate to help him forget what he was doing. Because as soon as I start kissing him, I discover I have no intention of stopping, at least not any time this witching hour.

I slide my hands up his chest, and Evengi lets out a sigh, and then he is kissing me back, his hands on my hips, gripping into the sides of my dress.

As I lean closer, tracing my lips over his, suddenly a chilling neigh echoes through the forest. Evengi shoves me away, coming to his senses first, and I stumble back a step, almost landing in the squirrel remains myself.

He whips his head around. "We aren't alone in this forest," he says just as a dark form that appears to be mounted on horseback races through the woods, silent as the night.

CHAPTER TEN
NATASYA

How could I have been so stupid?

I don't know who saw us kissing in the woods, but if word gets back to Brom I'll have ruined everything. My entire plan is about to go up in flames and all because one too curious outsider almost walked in on me practicing necromancy.

Although the blame can't be exclusively laid at Evengi's feet. After all, I'm the one who thought I'd use my feminine wiles to distract him from that fact. I'm the one who *kissed* him.

"Idiot," I growl to myself.

There are easier ways to get rid of prying eyes. For one, I could always pluck them out. Not kiss and reward the man snooping into my affairs.

I press open the door to the cottage my father bought for me to use while I'm staying here in Sunder Hollow and freeze when I come across a note lying on the floor as if it had been slipped under the door. It has my name scrawled across it in Brom's handwriting.

My heart stops, and I glance outside at the quickly lightening gray sky. Did someone wake him up at the crack of dawn to tell him what they saw? I'd thought I'd at least have some time to figure out my excuses.

Although I'm not quite sure how I am going to excuse my behavior. I've been acting the same I was when I was utterly unattached. It's true that my marriage with Brom would be a loveless one, at least on my end, and very likely on Brom's as well. He may act doting, but I know full well that he doesn't love me. It's a fairly well-kept secret by the Lower Elves, but if they come to love someone and then lose that person, they do not handle the loss well at all. They would rather die than face an eternity without them. They die quite literally of a broken heart.

I only know because I was raised by a Lower Elf, and Elwis has spent my entire life worrying he would lose me, my sisters, or my mother and he would die from the loss.

He has given my twin, Bronwyn, and I time to live our lives as humans, but while we are given the choice to choose when we will become vampires, Elwis already decided for us that we *will* become vampires someday.

My mother Vala chose it when she saw her first gray hair, I intend to take my father up on his offer of immortality long before then. But for the time being I am enjoying the ease of a human life. I'm already an outcast as a necromancer, but as a vampire, I would be doubly an outcast. And this time visibly so.

Brom does not act like someone whose very life hinges on my survival. He sees me more as a prize, one that he won, and he is pleased about keeping for himself. Still knowing all this, I never intended to be *unfaithful*.

I place my hand over my heart as I draw to a stop. Dear gods and demigods alike, is that what I was?

I'd only been wanting to distract Evengi from my necromantic practices, but to anyone watching from the outside... to Evengi even, I was kissing a man who wasn't my fiancé.

I suddenly start wondering if maybe I really want to be engaged if it comes with this much expectation. It's true that it's the easiest way to get my hands on the spellbook, but there are other ways to get it.

I'm pondering those other options as I stare at the note on the floor at my feet as I try to come to terms with the fact that my engagement is likely over already.

I may not love Brom, but I certainly don't wish to kill him, so I will need to steal the spellbook from him somehow. That will not be easy, spellbooks are usually jealously guarded by their Magickers. And while Brom may be little more than a cheap illusionist, his spellbook is still very powerful. If he chooses to use any spells in it to keep the book from me well...

Once the wielder of that spellbook killed a hundred necromancers, so what good would I do against it?

I need to be smart, but first I need to figure out just how angry Brom is with me.

I bend down, picking up the note and unfolding it to read the message hastily scrawled across it.

My darling Natasya...

I feel my eyebrows rise. Apparently, he is not that angry enough with me that he would forego the terms of endearment.

I understand that it is late, but I have not been able to sleep. I did not wish to disturb you from your slumber, hence the reason for my leaving this note. Once you read this, please meet me at the old-gnarled oak at the crossroads outside Sunder Hollow. I have something of the utmost importance to discuss with you. Evengi Ichabod is not to be trusted. He is lying to this whole town. Come quickly and I will reveal all and then you and I can decide the best course of action for that lying scoundrel.

I lower the note, feeling my eyes widen in surprise. This has nothing to do with me at all, but actually Evengi.

Relief rushes through me, followed closely by a burning curiosity. Just who is this Evengi? It seems I'm not the only one in Sunder Hollow telling lies. I suppose it makes sense. The first man I've actually felt any sort of attraction toward, of course he must be a conniving liar himself.

I hastily throw on my heavy woolen cloak because the air has taken on a wet cold feeling. It promises a rain to come soon. I throw my hood up and hurry down the main road. There are very few people out at this hour. The blacksmith lighting his forge, the farmers heading to their fields, and me as I hurry down the dirt path to the wide road that cuts down through Ruskhazar. The crossroads that Brom referred to is the area where the road branches off to head to Sunder Hollow.

There's a broken sign that once stated that Sunder Hollow was up that road, but the path is mostly overgrown from misuse, and many people actually miss it when they walk this road.

Most people, except for Evengi apparently.

And me, but that was because I was purposefully seeking out Sunder Hollow. Is it possible that Evengi did the same thing?

It makes me all the more desperate to learn what Brom discovered about Evengi. Does he have ulterior motives for being in Sunder Hollow just like I do? If that's the case, then I can easily blackmail him and get him to leave before he further ruins my chances of marrying Brom the Bones and getting my hands on that spellbook.

I quicken my pace as I spot the twisted branches of the old oak tree that serves as a marker for the crossroads since the sign now lies rotting in the dirt, the words *Sunder Hollow* still etched into the wood.

This late in the year, the leaves are orange and red and seem to be barely clinging to the branches.

A gust of icy wind washes over me as I make it to the end of the path just where it becomes one with the main road. I don't see anyone around. Not lying in the tall grass, not pacing along the road, not perched on the rickety fence in front of the oak.

It seems as though I'm the only one here at this oak so early in the morning.

"Brom?" I call, pulling my cloak more closely around me as I glance up and down the main road in case he decided to wander down it while waiting for me. "Brom?"

No one answers my calls.

CHAPTER ELEVEN
EVENGI

To say that I'm confused is an understatement. I came here to free the restless spirits of the ghosts and perhaps hunt down a necromancer, not kiss someone's fiancé. Let alone *Brom's*.

My mother always used to say that we're more connected here in Ruskhazar than we realize and that this strife between Lowlanders, Highlanders, and Elves is ridiculous. But I'll admit that even I never thought I'd wind up finding my old friend Brom all these years later, let alone for us to both get involved with the same woman.

Natasya is a lot of trouble, especially for being just a merchant's daughter. How did she manage to get not one, but two lords, caught up in her snare.

How come I can't seem to stop thinking about that accursed kiss? It never should have happened, and yet, I can't help but be left wishing that I could recreate it. At least once more.

I pinch my nose and groan as the dim light of dawn flickers through the shuttered windows of my inn room. I'm behaving quite poorly for a man who has dedicated his life to the goddess Neltruna.

It's true her priests are not like most other priests; we don't worship in temples or preach of the gods power to the masses. No, we serve the goddess of darkness and monsters, and as such, it is our duty to display power over darkness and the monsters. Especially monsters, as many were created in defiance to Neltruna by her daughter Mavka, the demigoddess of night who wished to usurp her mother's domain.

The dragons were born of her daughter Mavka and the demigod Zudhac, the great and first dragon. Likewise, vampires were Mavka's cursed followers.

And my own specialty in monster hunting, ghosts, are a defiance against Neltruna's husband Thyre, who is supposed to be the guardian of the dead. These restless spirits have slipped past his grasp and choose to remain in Ruskhazar for whatever reason rather than go to Skyhold and enter into their eternal rest.

Many ghosts die violently and seek vengeance or are lost and confused not even having realized that they died or how. It's my duty to find them and convince them to enter Skyhold, either by avenging their violent deaths or by helping them to find clarity in their clouded confusion.

It's a sacred purpose that I have come to embrace since the gods chose to spare my life from that accident at the academy all those years ago.

On the bright side, the fewer ghosts there are, the less of a headache I have.

For instance, I have a pounding headache right now, and I blame half of it on the ghosts hissing and moaning all around me, the rest of the headache I attribute to Natasya and her kiss.

Someone pounds on the door, and I flinch, reaching up to rub at my forehead. I get to my feet wincing as they pound again, then a third time. I swing the door open, glaring. "What?" I demand.

Outside I find the older woman who I spoke to when I rented the room in this inn. She is ringing her hands as she stands next to a very bedraggled looking Natasya.

Fair Natasya's curly flame-colored hair hangs in her face, and her cloak is half hanging off her shoulders. The bottom of her skirts are stained brown from mud. But the thing that draws my attention the most is that she appears to be even angrier than I feel.

I feel my eyebrows rise to my hairline as she shakes a fist full of paper in my face. "What have you done to Brom?" she demands.

I'm so distracted by the fist being waved around in my face that it takes me a second too long to process her words.

"Brom?" I ask glancing from her to the innkeeper. "What's wrong with Brom?"

"That's Lord Bones to you," the innkeeper says with a huff. "And to think I gave you my best room, you person snatching fiend."

I fold my arms. "With all due respect, it was your only room." The best thing that settles for an inn in this small of a town is the backroom of the run-down tavern that had a few pieces of furniture thrown in.

The "innkeeper" narrows her eyes at me, but I turn my attention to Natasya. "Now what is it that you're trying to accuse me of?" I ask.

Natasya narrows her eyes, fire sparking through them as she regards me. "Brom is missing, not that I need to tell you that since you're the reason for it."

"That's a lofty accusation, especially since I know you have no proof," I growl, but even as I say it my heart drops in my chest. What does she mean that Brom is missing? Missing how? Since when?

I'm struggling to maintain my composure when Natasya thrusts the crumbled-up note in my face.

I open the note, my eyes skimming over the hastily scrawled penmanship. Finally, I look up at Natasya. "I don't know the nature of this note, I don't even know that it isn't a forgery to make me look bad, but I assure you I had nothing to do with Brom's disappearance. From the look of this note, it seems as though you would have been the only one to know where Brom was heading."

Natasya's mouth drops open. "Do you dare accuse me of my own fiancé's disappearance?"

"I'm simply pointing out the obvious," I say as I sweep my cloak over my shoulders. "But I intend to get to the bottom of this disappearance. You had best hope that I don't actually find cause to accuse you when I do."

I grab my bag, still packed up neat and tidy and toss the tavernkeeper a coin. "You can have your room back," I say, and then I nod to both the women and stride out of the room.

Something dark is afoot at Sunder Hollow and I intend to get to the bottom of it, and if I can happen to save one of my oldest acquaintances in the process, then the so much for it.

I know exactly where to start my search for answers because there is far more to Brom's bright eyed betrothed than meets the eye.

CHAPTER TWELVE
NATASYA

I could claw my hair out with my frustration. I let out a little shriek as I send the upturned drawer flying across the room before I turn to kick the gutted desk. No amount of searching through Brom's house has offered any clue as to where he has gone.

And worst still, it seems as if he had his spellbook on him when he disappeared.

I reach up, gripping the side of my head as I let out a little growl and begin pacing. Where could Brom be?

This is a small town and by now every inch of it would have been searched. He isn't hiding here in Sunder Hollow. There's always the woods and graveyard in the wilderness, not to mention a great big world outside this sleepy little town.

He could be anywhere by now and after hours of fruitless search I still have nothing more to go on than that single note.

I pull it from my satchel and crush it between my fingers. It's the only lead I have and it implicates one person. "Evengi," I growl. Fine, if he won't talk when I ask him nicely, I'll just have to make him talk by asking not so nicely.

It's bad enough that he took my fiancé from me, but to add insult to injury he took the spellbook as well?

The whole reason I am in this town is for that spellbook! I will *not* be leaving without it. I won't be the sister to fail my father, especially not when Bronwyn has already brought him a spellbook. I refuse to be shown up by my twin.

I sweep my skirts behind me as I stride from Brom's house, making sure to lock the door behind me with the spare key he gave me. I don't want any well-meaning townsperson meddling in there and finding something I might have missed.

It rained while I was searching Brom's house and my boots sink into the muddy road as I stride down the short path to my house. As the second finest building in town, it's situated near Brom's house in the finer part of town.

I open the door to my house busy contemplating where I might find that meddlesome Evengi Ichabod. He left his room in the back of the tavern, but I got the distinct impression that he wasn't leaving town.

So, where would he go?

I'm so preoccupied that I don't notice the chilly breeze until I'm stepping on the glass.

It crunches under my booted heel as I go completely still. My eyes dart to the window watching the cloth curtains rustle in the wind around broken jagged pieces.

I wave my hand, using my sorcery to sweep up the glass. I cause them to swirl around my skirts. I don't know who is in my house, but if they think they will reunite me with my missing betrothed by snatching me as well, then they have another thing coming to them.

They just broke into the house of a necromancer with far too much to lose.

I stride forward, walking slowly and trying to keep as quiet as possible. I'm afraid I lack the skills of my sister Corallin who possesses the exceptional ability to make herself as silent and unnoticeable as a shadow, but I suppose I can't have *all* the skills of the Eel family.

I press my shoulders against the doorframe and lean forward before I fully step from the entrance hall to the long dining hall that leads to the back of the house. To the right is the comely kitchen and to the left is my study where a staircase leads up past the second story where my library is and to the third story with my room.

However, as I creep past the long wooden dining table my eyes spot a door to the right of my hearth is slightly ajar.

It's the door that leads down into my cellar.

I silently curse as I race forward, leaving behind the shards of glass. That cellar is where I keep my dead things.

I hike up my skirts, tripping down the stairs in my hurry. Ahead I can see the orange glow of firelight as I reach the bottom of the steps. The cellar is a large nearly empty space with wooden beams holding up the ceiling and walls that are a mix of dirt and stone. The floor is fully dirt. The cellar door that leads outside is still chained shut.

Firelight dances off the pillars, emanating from a single torch held by a figure at the end of the space. I catch a glimpse of golden hair and a white streak.

"Evengi?" I ask, forcing myself to remain calm. I don't actually know what he is doing here or why, and I refuse to play my hand too early. Bronwyn always said I was too hotheaded to be the rational sister, but then again Bronwyn is usually wrong.

Evengi turns, and as he does, he steps to the side revealing a pile of gleaming bones.

I feel my eyes widen with horror as Evengi looks at me with accusation gleaming in his eyes. "What is this?" he demands.

One of the reasons that sorcery is so feared is because it is essentially the power of a demigod wielded by mortals, and it is not always predictable. Sometimes, it acts of its own accord as tempestuous and unreliable as the demigods the power stems from.

I've never truly had a chance to encounter this with my necromancy. I always thought I was just too powerful to lose control, but as I look at Evengi, the panic racing through my blood I watch with rising horror as the bones slide across the room.

The skull raises mounted on a hollow ribcage, one hand attaching to an arm and then the other as my father's remains raise all on their own.

"Papa," I gasp out, my eyes flying to the bones. Evengi turns at my words, and my heart drops into my stomach as he takes in the proof of my necromancy.

It's far too late to turn back now. My eyes land on a large rock near my skirt, and I snap my finger forcing my sorcery to take control of the stone just as it did the bones. I send it flying toward Evengi. It slams into the back of his head.

For a second, there is a moment of complete silence.

Then Evengi drops to the ground, his torch sputtering as it lands in the dirt. But the light, flickering and dim as it is, offers me enough light to stare into the face of the very big problem I now have to deal with.

CHAPTER THIRTEEN
NATASYA

I grit my teeth together, tightening my hold on Evengi's leg as he threatens to slip out of my sweaty grip.

"Put your back into it, Papa," I grunt out.

The skeleton clacks its teeth in return as if in protest. I roll my eyes. "This is all your fault. If you could have been a little less conspicuously dead, then we wouldn't even be in this mess."

My eyes dart down to Evengi's head as it lolls against his chest where he lays against my father's ribcage. Father has him under the arms, and I'm shuffling along behind him trying to hold up Evengi's legs. For such a skinny man, he is far heavier than he looks.

Unfortunately, my sorcery has no control over the living. I can only control soulless things such as the dead or inanimate objects. If I served a different demigod, I could have different abilities afforded to me, but I chose to serve the same demigod as my father and have the ability to manipulate the dead.

It's the most feared form of sorcery, but only because it's the most powerful. People fear what they can't control, and so they fear the dead. I have no such worries.

Forest leaves crunch under my boots, and I pause long enough to glance around to make sure that we are still alone. I couldn't very well leave Evengi in my house, so then I got the bright idea to drag him out in the forest and figure out what to do with him there.

Unfortunately, the dragging is proving to be more difficult than usual, and my father is *not* helping. I drop Evengi's legs and straighten, pressing my hands to my back. The skeleton continues on dragging Evengi along behind him but moving fairly slowly.

"You know, my actual father Elwis would be far more useful here," I scold the skeleton which lets out an angry clatter of teeth.

I roll my arms, stretching the sore muscles. "He actually has muscles and sinews." I'm having to use the force of my will to hold the skeleton together and keep it from falling apart under Evengi's weight which means that I'm having to exert double the energy just to move this frustrating enigma out of my cellar.

I hike up my skirt and stride through the forest, leaving behind the floundering skeleton. I find what I'm looking for beyond the next stretch of trees. The rolling burial mounds of Heretic's Rest.

A light mist hangs low to the ground, and a fence warns off those stupid enough to not realize that they're about to enter. A mass grave.

With the constant threat of necromancers turning the dead against the living, graves are usually isolated places tended by only priests of Thyre, the god of Skyhold, far from any towns. However, this particular graveyard is a place of pride and so Sunder Hollow was built just next to it.

Still, I am quite certain that I won't find anyone here. Even the people of Sunder Hollow don't stray too close to the Heretic's Rest.

The mounds are half grassy dirt and half built up with stones for support. Each has an opening that leads into the dark caverns beyond. The doorway is made of massive stones stacked on each other.

I turn seeing my father's skeleton struggling up to me, resolute in his task. I find his skeleton far better company than he was when he was living, at least I can admire the skeleton for never giving up.

If I give an order, it will follow it till it falls apart if need be.

I couldn't even get my father to give me a warm meal when I asked nicely.

"Just a little further, Papa," I tell it encouragingly as I duck my head into the burial mound. It's dark and dank, but the bodies here have been dead long enough that at least they don't stink. Normally grave keepers fill these mounds with sage and other herbs to mask the scent of decay, but no grave keeper has tended these mounds.

No one would do such a service to the corpses of necromancers. The only reason they were buried was to hide their bodies away to keep other necromancers from controlling them. I fold my arms, my eyes moving over the shelves lined with piles of bones.

Necromancers laid to their eternal rest. All their power over death and they couldn't save themselves from it.

I blink as light comes into the shadowy crypt and turn to see my father's bones shuffle in, dragging Evengi along behind him. Evengi's torch is wedged through my father's ribcage where I put it before we set out. I pull the torch out and gesture to the far wall. "Put him over there," I order.

Technically, I don't even need to speak to the skeleton. Speaking is how magickers control their magic; sorcerers are above such base need for control. We simply will it and it becomes so.

However, it makes me feel better to speak to the skeleton, makes it seem like he actually listens to me instead of being my unflinching puppet.

The bones creak slightly as the skeleton drags Evengi across the tomb. I glance around for a place to rest the torch but am drawn away from my task by Evengi's groan. He's coming too.

I feel my eyes widen as I look around for something to restrain him before my gaze falls on the two burial shelves Papa's skeleton placed Evengi between. As soon as the thought occurs, two skeletal hands swing out from their resting places and grasp Evengi's arms holding them above his head.

I smirk to myself as Evengi blinks his eyes open. Papa's skeleton shambles toward me and takes the torch out of my hand as Evengi glances around his eyes growing steadily wider.

"I'm sure you have some questions," I say brushing some dust off my skirts. "I know I do."

"You're a necromancer," he breathes. He pulls back, just then seeming to notice that his hands are being held in place by the skeletons in my control. He glances around at the crypt we are inside of. "Did you bring me out here to kill me?" he asks, raising a brow. He seems oddly calm for a man who thinks he is staring into the face of death. Almost as if he has seen death before and now knows it as a friend.

I cross my arms. "That depends, I suppose. On your answers to my questions." I step toward him, pausing above him. I kneel down so that I am on his level and brace my hand against the stone wall. I stare into his eyes, so clear blue even in the flickering dim lighting. "Where is Brom?"

"I assume in here somewhere." Evengi glances around with confusion. "Unless you did something else with his body."

I pull back, narrowing my eyes. "I didn't do anything to Brom."

Evengi laughs, actually laughs, and tilts his head up at me. "Forgive me if I don't take a practicing heretic's word for it."

I push to my feet pacing away. "No, you have him. You took him somewhere, and I will not let you go until you tell me where he is and that he is fine."

Evengi snaps his mouth shut and tilts his head as he studies me. "I'm not sure what mind games you are trying to play with me, but I won't give you the satisfaction."

"What is that supposed to mean?" I ask and at my words the skeletons tighten their hold on Evengi's arm.

He winces before he glances up at me, shaking his head to move his hair out of his face. "You're not letting me go, not now that I know your little secret."

I work my jaw as I stare into Evengi's defiant gaze. I'll admit, I'm not sure what to do with him once he tells me where Brom is.

I may play with the dead, but I've never actually killed anyone before. That's my father's and Corallin's territory. My mother always kept Bronwyn and I away from that part of his business saying we were too young to have any business killing.

I always knew eventually that would change; one couldn't remain too young forever. I'll admit, I never put too much thought into it.

I certainly never thought I'd hesitate when the time came to do so. I even have a good reason to kill him, to protect my secret and yet I can't help but find myself trying to reason out a way that I can get out of this without having to kill Evengi.

I could keep him here until I have the spellbook. Once I'm back with my family, I'll be safe from Evengi's accusations. Then he can tell Sunder Hollow all my dirty secrets.

But none of that will matter until I find Brom and make certain he is all right.

Then I'll have to figure out just what to do with this Evengi Ichabod.

CHAPTER FOURTEEN
EVENGI

I've run into quite a few situations during my time as a ghost hunter. Like the time I discovered a man had become a vampire by stumbling upon the ghost of the neighbor who was his first meal. Life as a priest of Neltruna has never been boring.

But I don't think I've ever experienced a situation suite like this.

I pull on my arms, testing what appears to be skeletal hands holding me in place. I count at least three resurrected dead which means I'm in the presence of a very powerful necromancer.

The dead are raised and controlled by the force of their will, so I'm not sure why I'm so surprised. If there's a word, I'd use to describe Natasya, it's willful.

She eyes me warily as she leans up against the wall of the tomb. I'm not sure what game she is playing in accusing me of making Brom disappear. It's obvious she's used him in some sort of dark ritual. I was right to suspect her. She's a necromancer after all.

But it begs the question of why she is putting on this act. Who is she hoping to fool? The skeletons?

I flex my fingers, deciding that my best chance of survival is to keep her talking. I'll be honest, I'm not sure why I'm still alive now that I know her secret, but it's probable that she needs a living soul to sacrifice to her demigod for more power or something equally evil.

Maybe it's the fate Brom had, but for now, I'm still alive, and I intend to keep it that way. I will not force the other priests of Neltruna to ship my remains back home to my parents.

"Why do you think I have anything to do with Brom's disappearance?" I ask, tilting my head.

She raises her brow. "Don't start playing innocent now. You broke into my house."

"Because I suspected *you* of Brom's disappearance."

"You say that now because you're worried of what I'm going to do when I find out that you killed my betrothed." She steps forward narrowing her eyes. "But that's nothing compared to what I'll do if you don't tell me where you buried him."

I can't help but snort. "In case you failed to notice you're the necromancer, if anyone is responsible for Brom's disappearance, it's you. What did he do? Did he find you out?"

"Was it jealousy?" she counters folding her arms. "Because you couldn't have me."

I snort at this. "Hardly."

She reaches into a pocket in her dress, pulling out the crumpled note which she holds up between her two fingers. "He knew a secret about you, something I would wager you didn't want to get out."

I roll my eyes. "It would just be an inconvenience I'd have to take time out of my day to explain away. I'd never kill a man over my true name."

Natasya raises her chin. "Let's see how much you declare your innocence after being trapped in here with the dead for a few hours."

I fold my legs. "The dead don't unsettle me. It's the living I find unpredictable."

She turns without another word and strides to the other side of the tomb. She won't go far though, she can't if she wants to keep her control over these skeletons. It's well enough, if she is here with me, I know that the people of Sunder Hollow are safe from her.

I turn, studying the hand gripping my arm. I yank on it to see if her will has broken in concentration at all, but it remains firm. I let out a sigh and rest my head back against the wall.

I wish I'd paid more attention during my time at the academy. Having a spell or two at the ready would be extremely useful at this moment.

But no, all I managed to do was pick up a little bit of runework and nearly get myself killed.

Something flickers out of the corner of my eye, and I turn to see a man standing there, staring down at me.

I start slightly, relaxing as I realize it's just a ghost. He's the first ghost to appear to me since coming to Sunder Hollow. It's a bearded man with deeply tanned skin and scruff along his jaw line.

"I see you've met my daughter," the ghost says as lowers down to sit next to me. He gestures to Natasya who is saying something to the skeleton.

"I do apologize for my part in kidnapping you. As you can see, my actions are not my own."

"Wait," I say in a low tone as my eyes lock on the skeleton. "That's you?"

The ghost purses his lips in displeasure. "Indeed, she insists on parading around my bones in this manner. My spirit cannot find rest with her flaunting my remains in such a disrespectful manner."

"Have you considered telling her that?" I ask as I watch her rub her finger across the grooves in the skeleton's skull as if cleaning out some dirt. It's obvious she has some sort of sick affection towards those bones. Perhaps if she knew how it tormented her father, she would stop.

"I'd never give her the satisfaction of appearing to her." He shakes his head with a grumble. "It's bad enough I had to tolerate her while I was living, but dead as well."

"What do you mean?" I ask, barely remembering to keep my tone low. "Don't you love your daughter?"

"*Gods*," the ghost says with a chuckle. "Of course not! She got my wife killed, and if that wasn't enough, she found a way to get me killed as well. Should have just left her to starve as a baby, her and that worthless sister of hers."

I whip my head to him, my eyes widening.

"I can't do anything as a spirit, of course, but now that you're here. Now that you can see and hear me..." the ghost trails off grinning widely revealing a few rotten teeth. "Well, now you can remedy that mistake. You can kill my daughter so that I can get my eternal rest at long last."

CHAPTER FIFTEEN
NATASYA

I pause, glancing up at Evengi. He is staring at something in the empty space of the tomb to his right. I don't know what he thinks he sees, but there is a look of mounting horror on his face.

I push to my feet, dusting off my skirts and stride toward him. "What are you looking at?"

Evengi startles, turning to me as if he forgot I was there. It's a little insulting actually. I'm holding him here with the bones of long dead necromancers the least he can do is not forget my presence.

"How long do you think you can keep these skeletons reanimated?" he demands instead as he turns the full force of those piercing blue eyes to me. "Maybe a few hours? A day? You'll have to sleep eventually."

"Don't you worry, Mr. Ichabod, I'm not in any danger of tiring out."

"Three skeletons are relatively impressive," he says although he doesn't sound impressed.

I bend over, bracing my hand on my knees. "I can do better," I whisper. "Oh, I've been reanimating my Papa since I was a child. It's quite literally child's play to me." I rest my hand on the skeleton's shoulder, leaning toward it. "After all these years it's nice to keep close to my father, don't you think?"

Evengi turns to that area next to him again and raises his eyebrow as if he is listening to something. He shakes his head with a snort. "You disgust me," he mutters.

I straighten. "Well, that's hardly fair. I'm actually a fairly nice person. I'm polite and unlike you I actually mind my own business. I only brought you here because you forced my hand."

Evengi turns back to me and gives his head a small shake. "Oh, I didn't actually mean you."

I pull up, glancing around in confusion. "And who exactly were you speaking to then? My father?"

Evengi's eye gets a twinkle in it as he smirks. "You could say that." I'm not sure how to respond as he folds his long legs and looks up at me. "Look, I think we got off to the wrong foot, and I'm beginning to lose feeling to my fingers."

I fold my arms as I step closer. "You're a lot less intimidated than you were before."

"I was never intimidated by you, darling," Evengi says. He tilts his head as he studies me. "Is it true that you've never actually killed anyone?"

I suck in a breath and stumble back a step, nearly tripping over the end of my dress. "Who told you that?"

"You prefer to let your father do your dirty work." He points to the skeleton. "Not that one. The living one."

I sneer as I pull back. "I don't know how you got that information, but clearly you're well informed."

"Not well informed enough to manage to avoid breaking into a necromancer's house. But I'm trying to remedy that by getting to know you now. I know now that the Natasya I met last night wasn't the real version of you, but I don't think this is you either. So why don't you put aside your ruses and we can discuss this civilly?"

I can't help but smirk at that. What a surprise that must have been for him? "You think you have me all figured out then?"

"Oh, no, I would never claim that."

I decide that it's time for a change in subject. "What were you doing in my home, planning to kidnap me in an attempt to get my father's money?"

He snorts. "As if I need your father's money."

"You're a vagabond," I point out.

"By choice." He sighs waving his fingers, I think perhaps he is just moving them to try to keep the blood pumping to them. "I was looking for evidence that you were linked to Brom's disappearance, but now..." He shakes his head. "If you didn't kill Brom, as I have been told you have never actually killed anyone, and you aren't currently holding him in this tomb, then where could he possibly be?"

I rest my hand on my hip, taking a half step back. "You say all this like you weren't the one who made Brom disappear."

"You didn't take him, did you?" he breathes.

"Did you?" I ask in return.

He flicks his gaze up at me, staring at me for a long moment as if trying to size me up. I wish him the best of luck, no one outside of my family, and perhaps Taryn, has never been able to see past the layers I have built up around myself to protect me from those who would hate me for who I am. "If I tell you the truth, will you consider actually letting me go?"

I arch my brow. It's cute that Evengi thinks he is in a position to make a deal with me, but then my father has always taught me to never underestimate a good bargain. Sometimes it's just easier than doing things the hard way.

Still, I can't just let him go, even if he has nothing to do with Brom's disappearance he knows I'm a necromancer. I need to keep him close until at least I'm able to leave town with that spellbook safely in my possession.

"If you tell me the truth, I won't harm you," I say at last. "I'll have no need to if I have the answers that I seek."

His eyes dart to the corner again. "You're not helpful," he says out of the corner of his mouth.

I feel my eyebrow rise even higher.

As he turns to me with a sigh. "I suppose that is better than nothing, and I'm just left to trust the word of a necromancer."

"If you won't trust the word of a necromancer, then trust the word of a lady," I say straightening.

Evengi's eyes flick up and down my form slowly. "All right, I guess that's the best I'm getting." He shifts his position so that he is sitting straighter. "It's true that I wasn't entirely forthright about my reasons for entering Sunder Hollow."

"I knew it," I declare smugly as I step away, I turn in a small circle and grin triumphantly at Evengi. "I knew it."

He is watching me with a somewhat amused expression on his face. As amused as anyone can be while being held in place by skeletal hands anyway. A strand of his chin length hair has escaped from its loose knot and is now falling into his face. Since his hands are otherwise occupied, I lean forward and push it out of his face.

This seems to startle him, and he looks up at me with surprise. I smirk at him. "It takes a liar to know a liar, Mr. Ichabod. And I knew you were lying almost from the start."

"To be fair, my secrets were not nearly as dark as yours, my fair Natasya." He smirks up at me. "I help people and serve the gods. You tinker with dead things."

"Are you going to get on with it or preach to me?"

"Why not a little bit of both?" He turns his hands so that they are palm up. "After all, you wanted to know who I am. Well, this is it, I am a priest of Neltruna."

I recoil at that. Evengi is a priest? Out of everything I'd expected from him this was certainly not it.

"Oh, how repulsive," I reply sticking out my tongue. "Am I going to be smote by the gods for letting you kiss me?"

"If you are to be smote for anything, it's for being a necromancer. I'm no more holy than any other person, I may serve the gods but I'm still just a man. Also, I'll remind you that *you* kissed *me* not the other way around."

I fold my arms, still not feeling comforted by this discovery. "Where are your orange robes?"

He smirks. "I thought they clashed with my complexion."

"So, you're a priest, but you're not very priestly."

Evengi shrugs. "I serve the goddess of darkness and monsters by hunting monsters with the rest of my order, not tending churches or grave sites. I, in particular specialize in ghosts."

Faintly I remember Evengi's comment during the dance about ghosts. I feel my eyebrows rise. "Ghosts?"

He grins. "I can see them better than most."

"There must be many ghosts here," I say glancing around at the shelves lined with bones.

"Indeed, and they are angry, but they won't materialize even to me." He does a double take to the corner. "Well, most of them won't."

I point to the corner. "Those comments you were making earlier when you kept saying you weren't talking to me, you were talking to a ghost, weren't you?"

Evengi hesitates for a second before he nods.

I reach up tapping my finger against my lip. If what Evengi said is true, I'm having a harder time imagining him being the one behind Brom's disappearance.

He may be a bit more blood thirsty than most priests and probably wouldn't hesitate to kill my family who are vampires, but what reason would he have to attack Brom?

"You really didn't take Brom, did you?" I ask with a sigh as I rest my hands on my hips.

He shakes his head. "And I only broke into your house because I suspected you of something nefarious. I was right, but I did misjudge just how nefarious you were."

"Flatterer," I say, waving my hand through the air. I pace to the side, pausing as I catch a glimpse into the adjoining tunnel that leads to further burial chambers. There is a flicker like torchlight within. I take a small step forward when suddenly Evengi cries out my name.

"Natasya!"

I nearly jump out of my skin as I whirl. "What?" I demand.

Evengi's eyes are wide and excited as he stares at the entrance of the burial mound. "It's Brom, I just saw him. He's all right. He just poked his head in here and then took off."

I take two steps forward, ready to race after my fiancé but draw short when Evengi clears his throat.

I pause and release a sigh. I can't very well leave him here. Necromancy only works across short distances. I could knock him unconscious, but that's an unreliable method I'd have no way of knowing how long he would remain unconscious or of making certain that he doesn't wake up before I return.

I jab a finger through the air. "Don't you dare even think about making a run for the village."

"I'm just as concerned with getting Brom back whole as you are," he assures me. "On my honor as a priest, we can have a truce for as long as it takes to ensure that."

"I hate the honor of priests," I mutter as I shake my head, but I wave my hands and the skeletons release Evengi's hands going back to being just as dead as before. I inhale deeply as it feels like a weight is lifted off my lungs. Now I just have to worry about keeping my papa reanimated.

Evengi pushes to his feet, gingerly rubbing his wrists. "All right then, let's go find Brom so that we can go back to being mortal enemies."

I give a sharp nod. "Agreed."

CHAPTER SIXTEEN
EVENGI

"**S**he was always such a willful girl."

I grimace as I step out into the daylight. I take back every wish I had that a ghost would appear to me in Sunder Hollow and tell me what was going on. I'd take ignorance over the company of Natasya's father's ghost any day.

From what I've managed to gather from all his ranting is that he utterly despises his daughter, which leaves me in the most unwanted position of having to feel sympathy for a necromancer. I mean, no wonder she turned out the way she did when her own father hated her.

I myself was blessed with the most saintly parents in all of Ruskhazar. They doted on me and my sister, only wanting the best for us. We were wealthy, well loved, and the world was at our feet.

And that left me bored. Who was I if I never actually had to work toward anything? I simply existed in this world, but I did not take part in it, not in any sort of significant way. It's why I was so restless in my youth jumping from one pursuit to the next until that fateful day in the Academy of Magickers where I nearly died because of my careless irresponsibility. Magic was a dangerous thing, and I was treating it like a hobby.

But due to that I found my calling.

A calling I still haven't managed to share with my family. While I'm satisfied with my role as a ghost hunter and priest of Neltruna, I know my parents would be disappointed. They would want more for me, and my mother especially would want me to finally have a family and start popping out grandkids for her.

Not exactly a lifestyle a nomadic priest would have. It's true that priests of Neltruna aren't necessarily forbidden from marriage, after all it was the gods who were the first to marry, it's just that life of a monster hunter is not without its perils, and many would not bring a wife into that life.

So, I simply didn't tell them. The fear of disappointing them was so strong that I traveled under a fake name and while I told my family I was adventuring I worked toward my higher calling.

All the while lying to the people, I loved the most.

If I'd died back there, if Natasya had been any other sort of necromancer, my parents and sister would never have known what became of me. I'd have just disappeared. Or the others of my order would have eventually found me and been forced to deliver news of my death to my family.

I'm not sure which would have been worse.

Natasya kneels on the ground studying the grass, probably looking for a booted imprint in the ground. Tracking is a skill that many priests of Neltruna have picked up, but not me. My prey is usually noncorporeal.

Like the ghost standing next to me, watching Natasya with a disgusted look on his face.

"She had it in her head even at a young age that she would go to the Academy of Magickers. 'I'm going to be a magicker, papa, and fight monsters,' she would always say," the ghost mutters, his voice taking on a higher tone as he mimics his daughter. He rolls his eyes. "As if I could have afforded to buy her magical equipment so she could pursue a whim."

"And supporting her would have been *so* terrible," I grumble, making certain to keep my voice low. I don't want Natasya to know that I'm defending her to her dead father. Although, I don't actually know why I'm hesitant. Do I not want for her to hear that I'm defending her and get ideas that I support her lifestyle, or do I not want her to know that her father is here and that he still hates her?

That he told me to kill her.

What a request to come from a father's mouth. Dead or not, how could he want that fate for his child?

I made that deal with her half to spite him.

"As you can clearly see, she never had a real passion for magic," her father replies dryly. "Actually, it was her sister who went to the Academy of Magickers. Bronwyn was always the far better daughter." He shakes his head grumbling under his breath. "And more obedient too."

Natasya straightens as she glances back at me. I rub my ear against my shoulder to try to drown out her father's voice. She wrinkles her nose in confusion. "Are you certain you saw Brom?"

"I think I'd know him if I saw him," I reply folding my arms. "Do you think I saw someone else?"

"I don't see any tracks other than our own here," she says gesturing down to the grass.

"As if she's an expert," her father says with a snort. "She forgets she's just a farmer's daughter. I wish I had control of my body so I could show her just what I think of her lofty airs. I'd choke the life out of her here and now, just like you should be doing."

I duck my head again. As I raise my shoulder to my ear, I catch sight of something in the tree line just outside the graveyard. It waves at me, and I realize that it's Brom.

"There he is!" I cry.

Brom waves more emphatically as if he is trying to urge us to come to him. I wonder why he doesn't come to us until I hear it. The shrieking whiny of a horse.

I turn to see a black stallion come out from behind a mound just a little across the burial way from where we are standing.

There's something off about the silhouette of the horse's rider. As he turns his steed toward us, I realize just what it is. There is nothing above his shoulders, just empty sky where his head should be.

I don't know what sort of dark necromancy is afoot, but that thing is clearly not a member of the living.

"What the Skyhold..." Natasya breathes just as the horse snorts and takes off after us, bringing its headless rider closer. I whirl, grabbing Natasya's arm as I race past her.

"Run," I say, and since she doesn't seem to react quickly enough, I yank on her arm again. "Run!"

Natasya whips her head around and takes off after me. I don't let go of her arm though. I hope somehow, I'm propelling her faster as I race toward the tree line where I saw Brom.

Behind me, I can hear the pounding of hooves and the heaving breaths of the steed.

The rider, however, is eerily silent.

I duck my head under a branch as we break through the tree line. I don't slow my pace at all. These trees won't stop the horse and its rider, but they can slow them down. And in the process offer us some cover. I don't know where Brom went, but I hope that he has gotten himself to safety.

I don't know what this headless rider wants, or rather what the necromancer that raised him wants, but I don't intend to stick around and find out.

I've already been held against my will by one necromancer too many today. I can barely believe that I'm still alive after discovering who Natasya really is, and I have no intention of testing my luck. Just because I somehow found the only non-bloodthirsty necromancer in all of Ruskhazar does not mean that I'll survive a second necromancer. Indeed, I fully expect I wouldn't.

And for that matter neither would Natasya. Necromancers do not tend to get along together. They see themselves as each other's rivals.

They are power hungry creatures and they do not like to see someone else wield that power as well.

A branch snaps against my cheek as I push toward the deepest parts of the forest. But I can't help but wonder how long we can keep this up. Natasya and I are both breathing hard. If not for these trees, the headless rider would have caught us already.

Just as I'm thinking this, Natasya tugs on my arm.

"There," she says, gasping out the word.

I turn my head to see that she is pointing to an old half rotten oak tree. Its roots are twisted and gnarled and form a slight hollow underneath the tree.

I slip in fallen leaves as I veer off course, heading toward the tree. I release Natasya's arm as we reach the tree. I turn glancing around wildly as she drops to her knees and crawls in ahead of me.

I can hear a whinny and it's close. I drop into the hole. I'm not entirely sure how I managed to contort myself to fit in the space, especially with Natasya there, or how I managed to do so as quickly as I did.

I likely scraped myself in several areas and I just haven't processed the pain yet, but at the moment, my world has narrowed down to the measure of my attempt to control my breaths.

Natasya pressed up against me, her chest is against my arm and I can feel her heart hammering against her ribcage like a frightened bird's wings.

The roots wrapped around us hopefully offer us enough shelter.

The black hoof stepped into view only a stone's throw from where we are hiding now.

I hear the sliding sound of a sword being pulled from its sheath and suddenly a blade lowers in front of us, hanging beside the hoof.

It's an old blade, broken and bent, but still sharp enough to cut and already stained in dried blood.

Natasya shrinks into my side, and unthinking, I wrap my arm around her shoulder, holding her close.

Suddenly, I hear a twig snap a short distance away. The horse snorts and then in a thunder of hooves it is gone bearing its rider and that bloody blade away with it.

"That's my papa," Natasya says in a proud whisper.

The ghost harrumphs reminding me that he's still there.

I push up, poking my head out of the burrow. Natasya grabs my arm, yanking me back.

"What are you doing?" she hisses. "It's still out there."

"And so is Brom," I say as I crawl out of the hole. Whatever is happening here at this mass grave, I intend to find him before that horseman does.

CHAPTER SEVENTEEN
NATASYA

I clutch my hand to my heart as I pull myself out of the crevice that Evengi and I had sought shelter in.

Evengi turns, holding his hand out toward me, but I'm already struggling to my feet, peering with trepidation into the forest.

"What's the matter?" he asks turning as if half expecting the horseman to be there just behind him.

"It's my papa," I whisper. "I cannot feel him anymore."

Evengi glances to his right even though there is only empty air there. He turns, clearing his throat. "I'm sure that your skeleton is fine, Natasya."

I nod, but as I do, I feel something moist on the corner of my eye. I quickly reach up, wiping at the tear and silently cursing myself for being incapable of controlling my feelings especially in front of Evengi. I need to be hard and cold like a stone, show him that I am not one to be messed with.

Not a sniveling shivering girl who is scared without her father.

"Hey," Evengi says as he steps towards me. He rests his hand on my shoulder. "It's all right."

"Is it?" I ask with a sniff. "I can't lose him. He is all I have left of my birth father."

Evengi once again glances at that empty space before he clears his throat. "He must have been an exceptional man."

I shake my head with a sniff, reaching up to wipe my nose. "He was a monster. He hadn't wanted us, and he made that utterly clear to us. My adopted father killed him because he saw how he despised my sister and me. My papa... he used to reward Bronwyn for beating me herself, so he didn't have to get his hands dirty." I reach up and dab at my eyes. Not that I blame Bronwyn, she was so young and just as scared of him as I was. We were both his victims. "That skeleton was my only chance to actually have a relationship with my birth father, and now I'm worried it's gone."

Evengi's face twists as he moves another step closer and then to my utter surprise, he wraps me in a hug. I stiffen as he pulls away, rubbing his hands up and down my arm.

"We're looking for Brom anyway, we can keep an eye out for your father's bones."

I would be able to sense it if we got near, especially since I am so attuned to those bones in particular. That's what scares me, I never should have lost my connection to him. My papa hadn't been that far away.

It's as if he just simply ceased to exist.

"There's no need for you to be nice to me," I say as I wrap my arm around myself and start forward. I glance through the trees making certain that the horseman hasn't doubled back and is heading straight toward us.

"Maybe not, but it makes me wonder how different your life would be if you had been afforded a bit of kindness in your life," Evengi says as he falls into step beside me.

"You really are a priest," I reply with a snort. "Don't try to see the best in me; you will only fool yourself."

"I think I already have," Evengi says as he glances at me, but he fails to elaborate on his cryptic statement.

I duck under a branch, peering around, but just as I lost my connection to my papa, I don't sense any other corpses nearby. Although since the horseman is already animated by a necromancer, I will have no power over it. It is no empty vessel so I can't sense it like I could anything else dead.

The sun has already disappeared, and darkness is falling upon the forest. Papa had the torch...

I try not to start crying again, the last thing I need is for this priest to decide that I'm a charity case. And yet, I don't feel nearly as disgusted by his pity as I thought I would. I'm slightly touched that he would even care. Least of all for a necromancer like me.

"Who do you think is controlling that horseman?" I ask, shivering slightly as a bitter wind blows through the trees.

"I was hoping you would know since necromancy is more of your area of expertise."

I glance at him over my shoulder, but I can only make out his silhouette now. "Necromancy, yes, but other necromancers? Hardly."

Evengi bumps into a tree and then curses in a very un-priestly way. "I assume a close family member of yours is a necromancer, they are the ones who taught you. You don't seem like you were brought up in a coven."

"Am I too refined for that?" I ask smiling. "But don't expect me to answer your question."

"It was your adopted father," Evengi says although I have no idea how he could have inferred that.

I whirl so fast that he nearly runs me over. I glare up at his shadowy face and jab him in the chest. "Threaten me all you like but if you breathe one word against my father, and you will never make it out of these woods."

"You seem like you are very family oriented," Evengi says sounding amused. It's frustrating, I meant every word of my threat.

I turn around, crossing my arms. "So, what if I am?"

"You mentioned a twin, are you and she close?"

"Close enough," I reply.

"And your other sister is a sorceress like you, but not a necromancer. She is, however, a vampire."

I whirl again. "Where are you getting your information?"

Evengi raises his shoulder, rubbing it against his ear. "I have my sources."

I turn around again, but I can't shake the unsettled feeling that has settled over me to hear Evengi speak of my family. My family is my own. I have no idea how he could have gotten this information, but we obviously have some security breach.

No one should know this much about the Eels save for us ourselves.

So how could Evengi? Just who is this priest and how does he know me better than anyone else outside of my family ever has?

CHAPTER EIGHTEEN
EVENGI

The ghost of Natasya's father is useful in one way, he is an endless fount of information when it comes to his daughter. It seems as though he has been haunting her since he died, and she began resurrecting his bones.

And now he has decided to unburden his soul by telling me everything he has witnessed. Perhaps he thinks that it will make me more likely to accomplish his dark purpose of killing his daughter.

I think the details he shares with me of her father's criminal dealings and how vampirism has tainted her family is supposed to make feel disgusted toward her. Disgusted enough to do what any proper priest of Neltruna would and kill the necromancer and kill her entire family of undead, criminal, heretics.

But in fact, it only serves to help me better understand this girl who has been an enigma since I came into Sunder Hollow.

She's just a lost soul who has been shaped into a heretic by her family. Not because she is evil but because she does not know any better.

Is it not my place a priest to try to lead her to the light? To save her from herself and the person her family made her.

The woman that Elwis the Eel created.

I ignore the fact that I serve a goddess of darkness. It isn't my duty to lead people to the light. It's my duty to hunt monsters.

But is Natasya truly a monster just because she is a necromancer? I know that she hasn't killed anyone, her father admitted it in one of his tirades. She's just a victim of her circumstances.

"And her summers she spends in the company of even more vampires," her father continues oblivious to the fact that I'm only half listening. "Even worse, the uncle of this closest friend is the most vile and powerful necromancer in all the land. I cannot believe my own flesh and blood would grow up to be such a creature." Her father sneers as he stares after her as Natasya makes her way through the woods. "It's why you must end her, think of the innocents you will save, and I will not have this guilt on my head."

"No, you'd rather I have the guilt of her life on *my* head," I say. I grimace as soon as the words leave my lips as I realize that I spoke aloud.

Natasya whirls on me. It's dark, but not dark enough to hide the determined set to her shoulders. "Who is here?" she demands as she steps toward me. "You say you can see ghosts, hunter, so tell me. Who is here with us? Who is giving away all my secrets?"

I pull my lip in between my teeth as I shift from foot to foot.

She stalks back towards me. I can feel the heat of her glare even if I cannot see it.

"Who, Evengi?" she demands.

"It doesn't matter," I reply as I try to step around her. "We need to find Brom and locate your father's remains. And then we need to figure out what we are going to do about this headless horseman."

She braces her hand on my arm, and I go still. "It matters to me," she says in a low tone. "Please, show me that I can trust you. My life already depends on your ability to keep a secret. Show me I'm not wrong to leave you capable of destroying me. I want to trust you. I want to be able to leave my fate in your hands. I don't want to take drastic measures..." she trails off as her tone becomes tinted with emotion.

"If you're worried about anyone finding out that you are a necromancer then you needn't fret so. I won't tell anyone your secret," I tell her. It may not seem like it with those hastily said words in the dark and damp night, but it's a solemn oath that goes against everything that I owe to the goddess Neltruna.

And yet, it feels as though a weight has been lifted off my chest as I say it. I don't want to be the one responsible for anything bad happening to Natasya. If that means I become guilty of harboring a necromancer's secret, then so be it.

"Prove it to me," she pleads.

Suddenly I'm able to place the emotion tinging her voice. Fear. She's frightened. And why wouldn't she be?

Her secret is out, her fiancé is missing, she's alone in the woods with a man who knows the truth about her, but she knows absolutely nothing about him.

And there's a headless horseman out there somewhere doing the gods know what.

"It's your father."

"What?" she demands sharply.

"I see your father's ghost," I say while the ghost hisses.

"Don't tell her that," he snarls as if I'd really listen to someone as despicable as this man. His hate for his daughter is partially responsible for how she ended up the way she is today.

"Elwis?" she gasps out as she goes limp. I surge forward, wrapping my arms around her to keep her from winding up on the forest floor.

"No, no, not that father. As far as I know, the criminal is just fine," I assure her even though I can't believe myself. It would be so much better for Natasya if her father were gone and no longer capable of corrupting her life. And yet here I am telling her that he's fine like that's actually a good thing.

"My birth father?" Natasya asks. She doesn't bother straightening but instead remains limp in my arms.

I press my lips together in a thin line. "I'm afraid so." I refrain from telling her that the only reason he is here is because he is tormented by her using his corpse in her necromancy or that he wants me to kill her. I'm not sure that's something she needs to hear right now.

A dry chuckle fills the air, and I look up to see Brom standing there a few yards away. He folds his arms as he studies me. "Look at you two. You seem so cozy there. I've only been gone for what? A day? And you're already moving in on my fiancée. I expect better from you, Ivan."

I straighten as I look up at him. "Brom?" I ask in surprise. "How long have you been here?"

Natasya pushes away from me, glancing around wildly. "Brom is here? Where?"

I raise my arm to point at him. "He's right..." I trail off as I look at Brom more closely. Despite the darkness of the forest and that I can only make out the outline of my hand even though it is right in front of me, I can see Brom clearly as if it's the middle of the afternoon.

Just like I can easily see Natasya's father. As if he is in a world where light and dark does not matter.

There is a thin line across his neck and a trickle of deep red liquid running down his collar to stain his shirt.

"Oh no," I whisper. "Brom no."

He smiles but there is no mirth in the expression. "About time you figured out that I was dead. And you both will be too if you don't get out of here. You must get out of Sunder Hollow. And most importantly, get away from the Heretic's Rest."

CHAPTER NINETEEN
NATASYA

I whip my head around, searching for Brom. Evengi is
staring at a point that as far as I can tell is occupied by
only dead leaves and gnarled roots.

"Where is Brom?" I demand, taking a step toward the
space that Evengi is staring.

"Natasya," Evengi whispers he moves closer to me. I
watch him warily as he reaches out, but he simply clasps
my hand, holding it up between us. "I'm so sorry."

"What?" I ask. As I look at Evengi closely, I notice that
his eyes have a slight glow to them, proof of Higher Elf
ancestry in his blood. It offers enough light that I can see
the sympathy in his gaze. "What is it? You're scaring me."

"Brom is... dead."

I stumble back, yanking my hand out of Evengi's hold. "How can you know that, how can you say that?"

Evengi bows his head. "You forget, I see the dead."

"Is his ghost here?" I demand, turning in a circle. "Brom are you here?"

"He is and he isn't," Evengi says. "He is still in the spirit realm, someplace I can see into. But he has not crossed over fully into Ruskhazar. If he were to do so, then you could see him as well."

"And what is stopping him from coming here?" I demand as I twist my fingers around themselves.

"He isn't sure if he wants to reveal himself to a necromancer, or to the woman who lied to him for his whole engagement." Evengi tilts his head but then scowls. "I'm not sharing that part."

"What part?" I demand.

"That you didn't even wait until my body was cold before you were kissing another man," Brom says stepping forward as if he was coming from another room. His appearance is blurred and distorted as if I am looking at a reflection of him on the water. Likewise, if I focus on the tree behind him then I can see straight through him.

But still, it is Brom all the same, his straight hair tumbles down around his shoulders. He's dressed in the same clothes he wore to the party.

Evengi raises his hand to pinch the bridge of his nose. "I do apologize for that, Brom."

Brom holds up his hand, cutting him off. "I don't blame you, Ivan. It's her, she's always had a mesmerizing way about her. A way of controlling the living as well as the dead."

I fold my arms. "I think this is hardly fair. I only kissed him to keep Evengi from discovering my secret."

"You did such a good job at that," Evengi replies his tone tinted with sarcasm.

I whip my head to him, narrowing my eyes. "And who is Ivan?"

"We are getting off topic," Evengi says ignoring me. "You mentioned our lives being in danger."

"They may very well be over for all I know," Brom says with a sigh. "I do not know if you have the power to save yourselves, but I had to at least try to warn you before you shared my fate. I haven't the time to pass my message through Ivan, even if he had proved a reliable messenger."

"I'm not a messenger, I'm a priest." Evengi folds his arms like a petulant child.

I tilt my head as I study Brom. "How did you die?"

He grimaces as he reaches for his neck. "Please know that this is a very uncomfortable topic for me to discuss."

"Believe it or not, you aren't the first ghost I've spoken to," Evengi says as he steps toward Brom. "Talking about their deaths has helped many of them come to terms with their sudden and violent demises. And in turn they were able to find peace in Skyhold."

Brom shakes his head, a small smile pulling at his lips. "Peace doesn't seem like an option right now. I'd just settle for others not sharing my fate. Even if those others happen to be my traitorous former fiancée and my old friend who kissed her."

Evengi grimaces and I pull my lip between my teeth. I decide to focus on the former part of his statement. "Who did this to you, Brom?"

"Necromancers," he replies, his tone dripping with disgust. "At first when I realized that you were a necromancer yourself, I had to follow you for a while to make certain that you weren't in league with them. But it seems that you are not connected to them despite sharing the same terrible dark arts."

"I am my own agent," I say. "And I serve my own ends."

"If you aren't careful, you will serve the necromancers' ends."

"How so?" Evengi asks, taking another step forward. He raises his hand as if to protect me but then thinks better of it and drops it back down to his side.

Brom shakes his head, raising his hand to his forehead. "I don't know how the spirits you help can find peace reliving their darkest moment."

"How is Natasya involved?" Evengi demands stepping forward.

Brom looks up, his eyes although transparent and seemingly fading away before my eyes are awash in anguish. "The necromancers that killed me are not alive."

I draw in a sharp breath, whipping my head toward the graveyard. "Heretic's Rest."

He gives a solemn nod. "Indeed, they are the very same monsters that my ancestor Borus the Conjurer fought all those hundreds of years ago."

"How is that possible?" Evengi breathes.

Brom shakes his head. "You will likely understand it better than I, Ghostspeaker. It seems that their spirits have remained here all this time, hoping, dreaming of some way to get revenge on the man who killed them. My ancestor. Somehow these spirits used necromancy to reanimate their bodies. They... they took my head." He raises his hand to his neck where I notice that there is a trickle of blood running from a paper-thin mark across his throat.

I raise my hands to cover my mouth in horror.

"How is such a thing possible?" Evengi demands, glancing at me. "Ghosts do not have power to affect the mortal realm."

Indeed, even I find it difficult to comprehend. Everyone knows that necromancy is the living manipulating the dead. There are no accounts of the dead controlling the living. But also, there is a darkness seeping into the land. A wild energy that gives power to even my own summoning of the dead.

There is a change that I have long sensed, one that lends power to the dead and inspires strength in the monsters. Shortly before I was born the third era began, the gods ended the second era with the promise that this would be the era of the prophesied end of the living. That if we do not do anything to change our fates, that it will be the last era.

Those that once existed in the darkness and shadows are now emboldened. They call this the era of the monsters.

Things that were once impossible are now becoming a nightmarish reality.

And I say this as a necromancer who was raised by a vampire, who fully expects to someday become a vampire myself.

Monsters and the dead are terribly bad for business. But more than that, I will not have some dead necromancers putting on airs and thinking that they can really get away with killing my fiancé.

I don't care how long their spirits floated through Sunder Hollow thirsting for revenge. That was *my* fiancé.

I curl my hand into my fist. "Which is why they needed their old bodies for the task. The must have reanimated their own bones for their bidding."

"But how can they control them when they are dead?"

I press my fingers against my lips. "Every day the powers of the demigods grows. It is why sorcerers are becoming more of a threat." I turn to study Evengi. "The power of the demigods has always transcended death. After all, the demigods have been dead for all of history and yet sorcerers can still harness their power. What if Tilbor's power is so strong now that even the dead can wield it?"

I give my head a sharp shake. To be honest, I'm disappointed in myself for not realizing this sooner. Tilbor is my patron after all, the demigod of the dead. I should have realized that his power had grown so much that it had reached this point. But I was so caught up in my own personal sorceries that I didn't notice my own patron plotting against me as well as the rest of the living while he conspired with those that he always considered his dominion. The dead.

It gives credence to the voices of all the naysayers who have hated sorcery and made it illegal. They did not want sorcerers wielding a power that they did not fully have control over, always fearing what the demigods might be plotting even in death.

All my life I have scoffed at them, but now I wonder if perhaps I was the foolish one after all.

Brom's eyes are haunted as he looks at me.

"So, you're saying that your killers are actually an army of undead necromancer spirits who are using their dead bodies as puppets so that they can still have a control over the world of the living?" Evengi demands glancing between the two of us.

"I am afraid so, yes," Brom replies.

"Your spellbook?" I ask stepping toward Brom. I reach for his arm just as I have done on numerous occasions. Only this time my hand passes straight through his arm. I choke back the tears rising in my throat.

I may have never truly loved Brom, but I did care about him. I was going to marry him. I'd planned to spend the rest of my life with him. This is not the future I had envisioned for us.

Brom looks down at my hand as it passes through him and sighs. "It's still attached to my belt on my...body." He grimaces. "Even though the necromancers cannot actually use it, they are gleeful at the thought of Borus the Conjurer's great spellbook being in their control."

I pace away shaking my head. That is not good news, but I suppose that it was too much to hope that the necromancers would not recognize the spellbook that was their undoing. Even if they cannot use it, they will keep a hold of it.

Somehow, we must get it back from them. That spellbook may just be our only hope of defeating the necromancers. After all, it defeated them the first time.

"What became of me is of little importance now, there is nothing to be done that can undo it," Brom says, his tone heavy with sadness. "I'm here not for myself but for you. You need to arm yourselves and prepare for a fight."

"Why?" Evengi asks stepping forward. "What is coming?"

Brom's voice cracks as he replies. "*Me*, I am. And even now there are a hundred eyes of the necromancers watching you from the spirit realm. You can't escape them; you have to find some way to stop them before they fulfill their dark purpose."

"What is it?" I ask, glancing toward Evengi. "Why are they so intent on us?"

"Because they wish to be reunited with their bodies and achieve what they consider immortality by escaping their death. And in order to complete the ritual that will give them this power... they will need the heart of a necromancer."

Brom studies us just as I hear a horse whiny in the distance.

Evengi whirls at the sound but Brom keeps his gaze locked on me. "The still beating heart of a living necromancer. It's always been a trap, Natasya, Ivan. I only hope that you find some way to outwit them. Because I could not."

CHAPTER TWENTY
NATASYA

"I don't want to witness what they will force me to do next," Brom says, his tone broken. I blink as he begins fading away, the tree behind him becoming clearer and clearer till I can't even tell if he is still here.

"I'm sorry," his voice comes again, faint like a whisper.

"Brom wait!" I cry, but he is already gone.

I have so many more questions to ask, apologies to say, explanations to give. But he's gone.

The truth is, he's been gone for a while, I just didn't want to consider it. It was easier to blame Evengi because at least I doubted Evengi would have killed him. But that doesn't change the grim truth that Brom the Bones has been dead all along.

I raise my hand to cover the side of my face as I draw in deep panicked breaths as I stare at the pile of leaves where Brom used to be. Suddenly, someone grips my arms and yanks me around. Hard enough to jolt me back to the present moment. I find myself staring into Evengi's wide eyes. "My name is not Evengi Ichabod. My name is Ivan Fyodorov."

"Fyodorov?" I whisper the name as faintly in the back of my mind it rings with familiarity. I've heard that name before.

He pushes me away from him. "If I don't make it, find my family and tell them I love them."

I stumble back in surprise, nearly tripping over the hem of my skirt as I watch a large black horse break through the trees. Now that I get a look at it, I recognize it as Brom's steed. Only its eyes have a strange and unnatural glow to them.

My eyes travel up the horse to its headless rider. As I see it up close, I see Brom's tunic, the neckline stained with dried blood. The rider carries a sword that must have been buried with the necromancers. An ancient blade but still sharp enough to have taken off his head.

My eyes flick down to his belt and the leather-bound book strapped to it. Evengi wraps his arms around me and throws us back as the horse rushes forward. The sword swings through the air, only just missing Evengi's neck

We both hit the ground, but I barely have the chance to catch my breath before Evengi is scrambling off me and yanking me to my feet. He shoves me to my feet.

"Run, Natasya, it's your heart they want."

"What about you?" I gasp out. My mind seems sluggish with everything happening. I want to slap myself and focus, but I can't seem to jar myself out of the stupor of learning that Brom is dead.

He smirks at me as he picks up a large branch as the horse prances in a circle to come back around. He swings it around like it's a blade, and it's evident that he has a fair bit of training. "I'll hold it off while you get away."

I stumble back several steps as Evengi raises the stick to block the next swing of the horseman then the rush of clarity comes over me. He's giving me a chance to get away and I'm squandering that opportunity in my dazed confusion.

I whirl on my heel and hike up my skirts as I take off through the woods. I need to get back to my father, he will know how to proceed and how to deal with this threat of necromancers. He will have the men available to kill them all over again. Then we can take Brom's spellbook, and my mission here in Sunder Hollow will be complete.

And I'll just have to live with the humiliation that my sister was able to accomplish her task of gaining a spellbook, but I could not without needing help.

I hate admitting defeat, but even I am not mad enough to face off against a hundred necromancers.

But Evengi is...

I shake my head at that thought. Evengi just needs to survive until I get help. He's uniquely suited for it, perhaps he can reason with the ghosts.

"If you take one more step, I will command my thrall to kill him."

I skid to a stop, slipping on wet leaves as I turn my head to see a transparent figure standing only a short distance away. He has a long black cloak with the hood pulled far over his face, hiding most of his features from view but I can see enough to make out his slimy eel of a smile. And I happen to be an expert on eels.

"And something tells me you don't want that," he continues.

I narrow my eyes as I study the ghost. There's a possibility that he is bluffing. Even if he isn't I should keep going. I'm bolstered by the fact that it's actually what Evengi would want.

He would do anything to keep the necromancers from winning, even if it means saving my life. But there's a niggling truth telling me that isn't his reason for saving me. After all, if he truly wanted to foil their plans, all it would take is killing me.

No, I think he actually chose to save me. For whatever reason that I'm not sure I could understand even after I've lived a hundred years.

And that keeps me from taking another step forward and sealing his fate.

I don't know what sort of man would potentially sacrifice himself to save his mortal enemy, but I know that the world would be a worse off place if it loses someone like that.

So, instead of turning and running, even if it's what Evengi would want me to do, I take a step toward the necromancer's ghost instead.

I feel my eyebrows rise and a smile play across my face as I realize that the dead necromancers may have a bargaining chip in Evengi, but I have a bargaining chip of my own. Myself.

"So," I say as I pace in front of him. "I hear you like your necromancers living. It would be a shame if someone altered that."

I reach into my shirt and draw out a poison vial hanging from a chain around my neck. A gift from my father, something to defend me if necromancy ever came up short. I shake the content of the vial. "This is the venom of a dragon's tooth. It's lethal and a fast-acting poison at that. Good luck getting my heart to beat again after I drink it. I'd be just as dead as you are now."

The ghost hisses. "You're lying."

I pop off the lid. "Let's prove it then."

"Wait!" The ghost snarls as he holds up his hand as if he could actually stop me. "You would truly face death for this man?"

"Death has been my constant companion since birth," I spit out. "Do you really think I'd actually fear it?"

The ghost is silent for a long moment before he says. "I suggest an exchange then. If this priest's life is so valuable to you that you would trade your own, then prove it. Take his place. Come to the burial mound, and we will make a trade. You for him."

I press my lips together as I consider his words. They are layered with utter surprise. I can't blame him, I'm not entirely sure why I'm doing this myself.

I should turn around and leave now, abandon Evengi to his fate.

I place the lid back on the bottle. "I'll come to your disgusting burial mound," I spit out, hardly believing the words coming from my mouth. "But he had better be in one piece when I get there."

The ghost smirks. "Believe me, as a necromancer you would know that dismemberment can be messy and complicated, but that is entirely up to you."

CHAPTER
TWENTY-ONE
EVENGI

"You fool!" Natasya's father howls in my ears. I grimace rubbing my ear against my shoulder. "You had every opportunity to let her die and yet you sacrificed yourself for her? Your blood will join a streaming river of red she leaves in her wake."

"At least it will allow me to find some peace away from you," I grumble as I stretch my fingers, trying to bring some circulation to my fingers.

I only just recently regained consciousness after the apparent thrashing Brom's decapitated body gave me. I try not to take the defeat too hard. It's difficult to defeat the dead, no killing blow would stop them. No, the only way to stop the undead is by completely destroying them.

Incineration is the course that most choose when dealing with fighting the dead.

Unfortunately, I don't happen to have any fire on hand, and I was never a very good magicker. As proven by the fact that I nearly got myself killed with a flame spell of my own back at the academy.

"Do you really think you will find peace if you are killed by a necromancer?" Natasya's father continues. "You know surprisingly little for being a ghost hunter."

I roll my eyes as I shift my weight slightly grimacing at the pounding in my head. Not all of it is because of the ghost, just most of it. The rest is likely the result of whatever blow I received to render me unconscious.

I turn my head to see that we are underground. Torches flicker because apparently not even the dead can see in the dark. Or more likely, the firelight has to do with whatever ritual they would like to perform. Perhaps the flames are meant to consume Natasya as they rip out her heart.

From the arrangement of the stones, I'd wager that I'm in one of the burial mounds. A central one given its size.

All around the mound are shambling corpses of the re-animated necromancers. I can make out the spirits floating above them flickering in and out of existence as a constant murmur drowns at my ears.

I start counting the decaying bodies gathered around but then give up. If it isn't the full one hundred necromancers, then it's pretty close.

I'm tied up and appear to have been stuffed into one of the slabs where they kept the dead before the bodies got up and wandered off.

I swallow down my panic at the thought of being this far underground and the racing thoughts wondering if Natasya got away.

I don't even allow my mind to ponder over what the dead could possibly be planning with me. They kept me alive for a reason and I'm not entirely sure if I want to know what that reason is.

Suddenly the dead part to the side, like a stream parting around a river and to my utter shock they reveal Natasya standing there. She looks resplendent, her red hair a flaming halo around her and her purple dress clings to her frame. Beautiful and very much alive, but for how much longer?

She strides forward like she has nothing to fear. Even though she is entering a room full of dead bodies that fully intend to rip her still beating heart from her chest.

I strain my neck as I stare at her with horror. She is holding a vial up near her mouth, I'm not sure what the contents are, but whatever it is, it seems to have upset the ghosts. They begin hissing and snarling.

"All right, I'm here," she calls out loudly. "Where is Evengi?"

My heart sinks with realization. She is here for me. Out of everything that I considered every possibility of how this would turn out, Natasya having a crisis of conscience and coming back for me was not even on the list. I counted on her sense of self-preservation. Her selfishness. The fact that she doesn't let moral scruples stop her.

I counted on her to act like a necromancer.

But here she is, standing there surrounded by dead things so vibrant and alive. And ready to throw that all away for me?

Before I can fully work through the crushing weight of disappointment over her actually doing something heroic, rough hands reach onto the shelf and yank me out.

I find myself staring into the empty space above Brom's collar as he swings the sword out. I flinch but they simply cut through the ropes holding me in place. I stretch my arms as I turn to Natasya.

"What are you doing here?" I demand, but her eyes are focused on something in the middle of the floor. I look down, realizing that it's a skull, cracked with half the side of it collapsed in on itself.

"Papa," Natasya breathes as she stares at it. Even from across the crypt I can see the tears shining in her eyes. Her eyes flick up as fury floods her face. "You killed my papa."

"We will send you to join him," one of the ghosts says with a dry chuckle as two of the dead grasp Natasya's arms. They wrest the potion vial away from her and throw it to the side. It cracks and there is an exploding sound as flames erupt. They aren't huge flames, but they are so hot that I can feel them from here. They leap up to one of the corpses, and it lets out a hollow screech as the flames climb up it, consuming the dried flesh and burial rags.

One of the necromancer ghosts screams. "My body! My form!"

In the moment of chaos, I feel something bump my now free hand.

I look down to see the grinning teeth of a rotting smile and the hollow eyeless stare of one of the undead. It holds something out to me, a worn brown leather book.

CHAPTER
TWENTY-TWO
NATASYA

I'd staked a lot on the fact that the necromancers wouldn't notice one extra dead amongst their ranks.

I won't lie, I was seriously considering just trading my life for Evengi's, even though I couldn't fathom why I would. But as I stepped into the burial mound, I saw the corpse there. The necromancers, it seemed, could only control one corpse at a time in their weakened state of being mere spirits.

So, the necromancer who controlled Brom had left his body unattended for me to come across. I reanimated it, and then while I played the part of keeping the spirits distracted, I sent my dead minion to relieve Brom's body of its spellbook.

I look across the way to see Evengi staring down at the spellbook as it is held out to him by the rotting corpse I sent to him.

"Evengi!" I shriek as the two corpses yank my arms apart. Skeletal hands grasp my shoulders as they shove me to my knees. A third undead steps in front of me, raising a crude dagger over its head "Read the book."

He jolts at my word, grabbing the book. He flips it open, and I hear necromancer spirits begin to realize that I was nothing more than a distraction.

"No!" one cries.

"Stop him!" another cries.

But it's too late, Evengi is already reading out loud. It's a strange language that I don't recognize, the language of magic. It's not one that I hear often, magickers always speak their spells softly in the barest of whispers to keep others from learning and stealing their spells.

But Evengi isn't a practiced magicker, so he reads it out loud. His tone is lilting and almost hypnotic. But what happens next is truly breathtaking.

Flames begin flickering through the air, dancing and skipping over our heads. As I watch the flames take on shapes, I blink as a dragon made of pure fire flaps its wings it lets out a breath of fire and suddenly the smell of burning flesh fills my nostrils.

After having been dead for so long, there was not flesh left on most of these necromancers, but what was had been dried and preserved. Easy kindling.

Over my head, I can hear the necromancers shrieking as the dragon lets out a snarl and swoops down on another section of the dead. They swing at it with what weapons they have, but their swords just pass through the magic.

I find myself smirking at the irony. The dead thought they were unkillable, until they met something else that couldn't be touched.

Suddenly Evengi is leaping through the flames. He lowers his shoulder and slams into one of the corpses holding me. With their puppeteers distracted I'm able to yank my arm out of the other's hold.

"Come on," Evengi cries as he reaches for my hand, but I jump out of his hold. I surge forward, grasping my father's skull. I won't leave him here to be incinerated like the rest of the dead. Then clutching the skull to my chest, I turn and take off toward Evengi. I pass him as I race up the incline toward the entrance of the burial mound. I am gagging on smoke and the horrid stench of the burning as I make it out into the fresh air. Evengi erupts behind me, bent over and gasping for breath.

I turn to him, taking in his soot-stained cheeks before I let out a squeal and throw my arms around his neck. Evengi is taken aback but to his credit rights himself easily. He lets out a laugh as he wraps his arms around me and spins me around.

"We made it!" I gasp out.

"That's a surprise."

"You had me worried, you idiot," I say as I lean forward and press a kiss to his lips. He stiffens under me, and I start to pull away ready to blame it all on the chaos of what happened but then suddenly he is tightening his arms around me. He loses his balance, and we both fall into the stone wall of the burial mound. He chuckles against my mouth as he raises a hand to run through my hair. Then he presses his lips to mine and kisses me back. He kisses me in a way that Brom never did, it sends warmth curling through my stomach, and I feel it all the way to my toes as he moves his lips against mine as if he is trying to memorize their every curve and angle.

He pulls back, arching a brow as we both gasp for breath. "Next time I sacrifice myself for you, do me a favor and don't try to make it in vain next time."

"Oh, never," I say with a laugh. "If you're stupid enough to try to sacrifice yourself for me again then I'll be just as reckless next time around. I will have you know that I am not in the business of accepting sacrifices."

The laugh dies on my lips as I spot the spellbook lying there in the grass. Discarded by Evengi when he caught me. I slide out of his hold and bend over, picking it up. I study the worn cover, flicking ash off the cover.

All that trouble just for this little book?

I will admit that if what Evengi did as an untrained Lowlander was anything to go on, this spellbook is invaluable. He conjured a flame dragon that killed a hundred dead.

My father will be unstoppable with this spellbook in my sister's hands. As official magicker of the family, Bronwyn will know how to wield these spells.

I hold the book close to my chest as I turn to the mound. "The spirits of the necromancers are still out there."

Evengi lets out a sigh as he steps toward me. "There are always spirits out there. The important part is that we defeated them."

I glance at him out of the corner of my eye. Is that really what is important?

Because I feel no giddy sense of accomplishment for having outwitted them nor do I feel relief to be holding the spellbook.

I just feel hollow while at the same time strangely filled.

So many have died. The necromancer's bodies suffered a second death, Brom has died, even my own Papa's bones are gone.

And yet, Evengi is not one of the dead, and for that, I am infinitely grateful.

CHAPTER TWENTY-THREE
EVENGI

I t's finally over, and yet I can't help but feel that perhaps *beginning* is the best way to describe this moment.

"You did it." I startle, whirling at the voice to see Brom standing behind me. His loose hair floats in a wind that is not here, and a small smile pulls at his lips. He has his hands clasped behind his back, looking far more relaxed than he had been the last time I saw him.

I know that look. There's a certain peace that most spirits find when they know that their killers will not harm anyone else.

He is studying Natasya who is kneeling at the burial mound, saying a final farewell to her father's bones and to

Brom. He looks at me out of the corner of his eye. "Please don't make a sound. I don't want her to know that I'm here. She would want me to come over back into this realm so she can see me, and I don't want a messy goodbye."

I nod.

"I think I found that peace you were speaking of," he says with a sigh. "There's just one last bit of unfinished business."

I raise my eyebrows in a silent question.

"Her," Brom says with a nod to Natasya. "I did love her, you know. Even if she is a necromancer, I still want to see her happy, but that happiness is not something she will find on her current path or with her family." He turns to me, his dark eyes holding me spellbound. "Please promise me you will take care of her. Help her to realize that she doesn't have to be the monster her circumstances have forced her to become."

I flick my gaze to Natasya as she bows her head. Her shoulders shake slightly, and I wonder if she is crying silently. Just as I am having a silent conversation.

"Take care of her because I cannot anymore. I long for peace, I long for Skyhold, and to see my ancestors, but I cannot do that unless I know she will be all right. That you both will be."

I hesitate only a second before I give a firm nod. I pray that my eyes convey what my mouth cannot. *I swear.*

I mean it with every fiber of my being. I know that I cannot just go back to my life knowing that she is out there drowning in darkness. As a priest of Neltruna, it is my duty to defeat monsters and drive away darkness. How can I go back to simply hunting for ghosts when my greatest challenge lies ahead of me?

To defeat Natasya's inner monsters and drive away the ghosts that haunt her every step.

Even if it takes my whole life, even if it destroys me, I will fight for Natasya and the goodness inside of her. I've seen it for myself now. She is selfless in a way I have not seen in many. She is clever and witty, and it isn't fair that she should be a demigod's pawn. I will get her away from her father and all others who would attempt to stain and mar her soul.

I'll save her from herself.

Not just for her or for Brom, but for me. I cannot allow this woman that I have come to care for, perhaps even love, to fall prey to the very thing I'm sworn to destroy.

"Thank you," Brom says exhaling in relief. He glances toward Natasya again. "Live a long, good life, Ivan, the both of you. Be happy, be in love, be everything I had taken from me by my untimely death."

I nod once again as Brom fades away. As he disappears, it is as if the air clears a little bit, like a presence in it has departed. He's gone, for good this time. I pray that he finds his peace in Skyhold.

I only wish that I could be rid of her father so easily. I turn to where he is there, always lingering on the sidelines. "So, you'll continue to be a part of her life," he murmurs. "*Good.*"

I roll my eyes and do my best to ignore him just as I am quickly growing accustomed to.

"I will haunt you, boy, for the rest of your miserable life. And with my daughter you will be miserable." I take a step toward her but draw up short when he materializes in front of me, his eyes crazed. "I'll drive you mad until you have no recourse but to finally kill her just to be free of me."

I draw in a deep breath and force myself to walk through her father's spirit. He lets out an indignant cry, but if he is speaking the truth, and he intends to haunt me until I kill Natasya then he will be haunting me for a very long time. I'll just have to get used to it and practice the art of drowning him out.

I raise my shoulder, rubbing it against my ear as I turn toward Natasya. I step forward and drop to my knees beside her. She reaches up, swiping at her eyes proving that she had indeed been crying, but she seems to wish to hide it, so I respect her wishes and pretend that I didn't see it. I instead rest a hand on her shoulder.

"I should never have come to Sunder Hollow," she whispers as she stares into the crypt to the shattered skull resting in the center of it with the flowers in its remaining eye socket. Brom's body is long gone, burned up with the rest. "If I hadn't none of this would have happened. Brom wouldn't have..." she trails off, unable to finish the sentence. She tightens her hold on the spellbook clutched in her hands. I still don't know all her reasoning for coming in the first place, but I've figured out enough that she was sent by her father and that spellbook had something to do with it.

As long as she is around her father, she will never be able to make a choice like the one that would have kept her from coming to Sunder Hollow. Because she is caught too deep in her father's snares. She would do anything that he asks of her, even put herself in danger just for a book of spells that she can't even use.

I clench my jaw but don't say what I am thinking out loud. Instead, I squeeze her shoulder gently. "It wasn't your fault. He loved you; you know?"

She reaches up quickly swiping her eye. "We never had the chance to be wed, our spirits will not be joined in my death."

"Would you have rather you were?" I ask, my heart caught in my throat. It's true the belief is that marriage exists even into death, that if one spouse dies, they will someday be rejoined with their lover in Skyhold to be together forever. Due to this belief, many who are widowed do not remarry because to do so is to break the ties with their former spouse and to give up an eternity with them.

Did she truly love him enough to wish to be with him for all eternity? If so, I'm not certain I have any chance with her if her heart truly burned with Brom.

"No, I suppose not," she says in a small voice, and with those four simple words I'm suddenly filled with hope. "But I do wish for some way to feel connected with him."

"You have his spellbook," I say resting my hand on the book clutched to her chest.

She draws in a deep shaky breath. "I lost a fiancé and a father all in one day."

"I'm sorry."

"Evengi," she whispers glancing at me out of the corner of her eye. "I mean Ivan," she hurriedly corrects.

"What is it?" I ask gently.

She fingers the book, glancing at the ground. "There is something I need to tell you although I don't know if I have the heart for it.

"I will have the heart for the both of us," I promise, shifting in the dirt to lean toward her.

Her eyes fill with tears at my words. "Then my heart will wind up broken all the same."

"What is it?" I ask, raising my hand to cup her cheek. She blinks and a tear spills over her lid, coursing down her cheek.

"It's your family, Ivan. I have heard the Fyodorov name before. My father was paying special attention to them because they had just secured a marriage alliance with the crown prince. He wanted to know more about the woman who would one day be queen."

I pull back in surprise. Alya is to be wed? To the crown prince? Indeed, I have missed much during my journeys as a lowly priest if that happened. I'm surprised my sister would ever allow such a thing, but I'm not sure why Natasya seems so upset over this news. It is startling, yes, but hardly the tragedy she is making it out to be.

"They were killed," she gasps out. "Assassinated."

I'm on my feet, stumbling back, but it's as if my head has become disconnected from my body as I listen to her words. Natasya crawls forward, clasping my leg which she rests her head against as if she isn't strong enough to hold it up. "It wasn't my father, I swear. It was an assassin group that operates outside of his jurisdiction, one specifically utilized by the Circle of Notability. The honor killers of the Order of the Bloody hand."

Her words are falling on deaf ears.

My family is dead.

Here I was, wandering over hills and across mountains, hunting ghosts and serving the goddess of monsters under a fake name, and all the while I was unreachable to my family. They were killed and I wasn't there for them.

I wasn't there to share their fate.

I didn't even know.

Oh, gods, my family is gone.

CHAPTER TWENTY-FOUR
NATASYA

I'm not sure if this was a good idea, but it's too late to turn back now.

I turn in a small circle as I take in the empty hall. So, this was the place where Evengi grew up? It's a beautiful manor with vast expanses and intricate stone carvings and woodwork. His family was obviously very powerful and wealthy.

And all dead now.

I may not be able to see ghosts the same way Evengi can, but I can sense something haunting him.

He strides down the center of the hallway, his head tilted at an odd angle as if he is looking into another world.

Although I have no idea if this world is the spirit realm or the past.

"My sister's name was Alya," he says his voice heavy. "She was four years younger than me. I was her older brother. I should have protected her. My mother... my father," his voice chokes off.

"My father has long suspected the crown prince of being behind the assassination," I say stepping toward a suite of armor standing on display in an alcove. I wipe my finger across the dark wood stand and study the white dust staining my fingertip. I look over to him. "The crown prince may seem unreachable, but my father can make him pay. He *will* make him pay if that is what you want."

He stares ahead of him, but his eyes are distant. I doubt he is seeing anything. I wonder if he even heard me. "Their ghosts never came to find me. Do you think that they are at peace?"

"If they weren't, you would have seen them and then helped them," I assure him. "But since you have not seen their ghosts that means they are in Skyhold."

He doesn't reply. Just stands there clenching and un-clenching his fist, a muscle in his jaw twitches slightly.

"Ivan?" I whisper.

"Ivan Fyodorov died with his family," he says at last. "Only Evengi remains."

"For what it's worth, I like Evengi Ichabod just fine."

He presses his eyes shut, but a tear slips down past his cheek.

"Oh Evengi..." I say. I step toward him, wrapping my arms around him from behind, pressing my cheek against his shoulder. I hold him tight as if with my arms alone I can keep him from shattering to a million pieces.

I know that it won't work though. I've been orphaned before, and that loss was a man I hated.

How much more would it hurt to lose the family that I have now? One that I love more than my own life? My father? My mother? My sisters? It would destroy me.

And I know that it is destroying Evengi now.

He lets out a ragged sob.

"I'm so sorry, I'm so sorry," I repeat over and over as he cries. I know that mere words are useless. I don't realize that I'm crying as well until I pull my face away and realize that the fabric of his tunic is soaked with my tears.

He turns into my embrace and wraps his arms around me. Somehow, we both wind up on our knees, each of us crying for our parents and the lives we will never have. I don't know how long we stay there with our arms around each other, both breaking and healing at the same time before Evengi finally releases a heavy breath. "Natasya?" he asks, his voice heavy with emotion.

I look up at him, blinking past the tears still pooling in my eyes. He leans forward, pressing a kiss against my forehead. He leaves his lips there for a long moment before he says. "Take me to see your father."

CHAPTER TWENTY-FIVE
NATASYA

I can't help but laugh when I see the look of utter surprise on Evengi's face. "What exactly were you expecting?"

He blinks once, then twice before he shakes his head. "Well, you told me your father was a vampire so perhaps a deep cave or an abandoned mine shaft somewhere. Maybe a mill or cabin in the middle of nowhere where he could practice his necromantic arts in solitude. Or even a long forgotten burial mound."

I giggle as I smack his arm. This is one of the things I think I love most about Evengi. He has such a black and white view of the world. He's so naïve and idealistic, it's sweet. "We are a family of vampires, sorcerers, and criminals. Whatever made you think we wouldn't be living in comfort?"

"And maybe if you were living in a grand palace, I could understand even that, but this?" Evengi blinks at the comely inn unable to tear his eyes off it as if it has cast a spell around him. The streets outside are already dark and an inviting glow comes from the paned windows. The sound of laughter and stringed instruments filters out from the inn.

The inn is built of wood with intricate carvings etched into every pillar and arch. The roof has been recently replaced, no longer made of thatch but made of shingles, something that is all the rage in the capital buildings. I think it makes it look more sophisticated.

I'd say that it rivals even the grandest great hall in the Highlander villages along the mountains, and although it's certainly not as large as the Lowlander manors it has twice the charm. So, I can't say I can see where Evengi's surprise is coming from.

The town where it resides is certainly not the largest, but its central location makes it so that it sees more than its fair share of travelers. This village was where my mother grew up dreaming of one day owning an inn of her own. And then she met my father who made sure to make her dream come true. All it cost was the life of the previous owner of the inn.

But she was the one who refused to sell it to him.

Over the course of their marriage my father and mother have fixed up the inn, adding to it and fitting it with fineries that can't be found in most inns. There is no inn in the land that can rival this one. Especially since sabotage is one of my father's preferred ways of dealing with competition.

It's a hobby of his, traveling Ruskhazar and making sure that my mother carries the reputation of having the finest inn in all the land. It just comes at making sure that the other inns all have a terrible reputation.

I turn to Evengi, tilting my head. "Well, are you planning on staying out here all night?"

Evengi swallows, doubt dancing across his blue eyes. "I just don't know about this."

I wrap my arm around his. "Come, you must meet my family sooner or later. Especially since if you don't properly introduce yourself to my father, he is liable to hunt you down."

Evengi presses his lips together, not looking too convinced.

I am about to tease him, but as I watch his neck work and glance down to see how tightly he is clenching his hand into a fist I realize that he is far more nervous about this than he is trying to let on. I step toward him, wrapping my arms around his waist. I rest my chin on his arm as I look up at him. "I promise it really isn't as bad as it seems from the outside. We may be criminals and some of us are undead, and some of us toy with the undead, but underneath all that we are just a family. So just look at them as my family. My father and mother and sisters and Wilder."

"Remind me, which of your sisters has this Wilder?" Evengi says. I've been going over my family with him, I don't know if he wants to make sure to know what he is up against or if he just wants to make sure he doesn't get anyone mixed up, but I find it quaint when he is so studious.

"My twin Bronwyn," I say. "Corallin is the Higher Elf and she's a—"

"Vampire," Evengi says with a nod. "Just like your father and mother, but you and Bronwyn aren't vampires."

"Yet," I reply which causes Evengi to clench his jaw.

I slide my hand down his arm, caressing his muscles before I place my palm against his. "Well, it's not getting any warmer out here. What do you say that we go inside where it's cozy?"

He exhales before he nods once. "I suppose I have to meet the Eels one of these days."

"Today is as good a day as any for new beginnings."

He hesitates a second before he shakes his head. "And I'm not going to be able to convince you to run away with me?"

"You'd best keep that talk to yourself while we're in the inn," I say angling my arm to elbow him without releasing his arm. "Although my father would probably be amused more than anything that you think you can find a place in Ruskhazar where you will be able to hide from him if you took his little girl away. But come on, we will be out here until the dawn if you had your way. And don't you know, night is the best time to meet a vampire." I wink at him and take a step toward the inn and the sound of stringed instruments and the bard singing mother's favorite song.

Evengi might not think it yet, but this will be good for him.

CHAPTER
TWENTY-SIX
EVENGI

I find myself wondering how one goes about bringing down a criminal empire.

Slowly.

As I hold out my hand to clasp Natasya's father's I decide that such a thing must be done slowly. First, I need to gain Natasya's trust and convince her that this is the right thing to do.

With the pain of losing my own family still fresh on my heart, I know that I cannot make her go through that as well. I would only succeed in getting her to hate me forever, and I can't very well save her soul if she hates me.

No, I have to make this something that she wants. And if I'm to do that then I will have to play a long game.

Staying by her side and biding my time.

But that doesn't mean that I have to like it. The more I learn about her father's criminal doings, the more disgusted I become. To lead a group of assassins?

Natasya assures me that those assassins weren't the ones to kill my family, but it makes no difference to me. To kill for money is a heartless thing.

Natasya's father eyes me, his gaze is deep red, a telltale sign of his vampirism. He is a cunning man, and it makes me wonder if he isn't seeing too much as he looks at me.

Toward the front of the inn a bard is singing the legend of Lord Taliz, but back in the kitchens we have ample privacy as Natasya begins running through the introductions to her family.

"This is my papa, Elwis the Eel," Natasya says resting her hand on her father's arm. He finally pulls his gaze away from me long enough to smile at her.

I will admit, even knowing that they were a lot of vampires, sorcerers, and murderers, her family is nothing like I expected. For one, her father is a Lower Elf. His people usually consider themselves superior to everyone else living in Ruskhazar. They look down on the Highlanders and outright despise the Higher Elves. They occasionally tolerate Lowlanders, but for the most part stick only to their own kind.

And even then, from the outside it appears that there is not much love felt between families. But Elwis not only seems to dote on his family, also has a member from each of the divided peoples of Ruskhazar.

His wife Vala, who Natasya introduces me to next, is a Highlander. She's a tall woman with short red hair that she wears adorned with a few small braids, in the manner of her people. She's the one who owns the inn. It makes me wonder how an innkeeper ended up married to an assassin lord, but I suppose I'll learn the story eventually.

Natasya steps toward a girl who has thick brown hair that she wears swept back. Despite the fact that the girl's hair is brown and Natasya's is fiery red, their hair carries the same soft curl. Their features are also extremely similar, with them both having strong brows, full lips, and a slightly turned up noses. This must be Natasya's twin.

"That's my Bronwyn," Natasya's father's ghost says just as I draw that realization. "She was always the better of the two, at least she knew when to keep quiet."

I clench my jaw slightly, refusing to look into the corner of the kitchen where he is standing just behind a Lowlander cook, dressed in a stained white outfit with an unsettling glint in his eyes.

"This is my twin Bronwyn," Natasya says, unaware that her father already introduced us.

Bronwyn eyes me up and down, twisting her mouth as she studies me. I flex my fingers as I force myself not to squirm under her gaze.

"You're certainly not what I expected my sister to bring home, but if you make her happy, I suppose you are fine by me."

The double edge of her statement is clear, if I make her sister unhappy then she will have a problem with me. Something tells me, that's not something I want to happen.

A young man pushes off from where he was perched on the large wooden table in the kitchen and offers me a charming smile as his ruby red eyes twinkle. He has white hair and pointed ears speaking of a Higher Elf heritage. That's something that we will have in common, I suppose.

"I'm Wilder," he says, his hand is cold as it clasps mine.

A vampire.

I smile as I turn to the final member of the family. This one is a full-blooded Higher Elf with gray blue skin and glowing eyes, although these ones glow red. Her white hair is swept up in a bun and she's dressed all in black.

"And this is Corallin," Natasya says.

The other sister is also a vampire, and if I recall correctly an assassin as well.

She doesn't say anything, so I don't bother either. Instead, I turn my attention back to Elwis the Eel and nod my head. "And I'm Ivan Fyodorov."

"I'm aware," Elwis says ominously.

"But please call me Evengi," I continue, trying not to allow him to phase me.

Vala smiles, warming the room immediately as she steps forward. "Our Natasya has already told us so much about you. We're ecstatic to meet the man who has stolen our girl's heart."

"Not stolen," Natasya says with a laugh as she slips her fingers through mine. "Willingly given."

I straighten at that, her words warming me to my very soul and reminding me of the importance of my task.

Saving this exceptional woman who I have come to love from herself and from her family's clutches.

I notice Elwis watching me again, his face is expressionless so I have no idea what he is thinking, but I'm certain that I wouldn't like it. He's a cunning one, it will not be easy to do anything without him noticing. But for Natasya I would take any risk.

Vala tells the creepy looking cook to serve up the best venison and I find myself smiling and attempting to make nice with Natasya's family.

For now, I will play my part and bid my time to win over Natasya's soul. After all, it turns out I'd do anything for that girl. Even put up with both her fathers haunting my every step.

EPILOGUE

E lwis suspected the boy of ulterior motives.

He sneered from his balcony-like platform built off the upper rooms that overlooked the rest of the inn where he oftentimes enjoyed sitting. And Natasya had brought this boy straight to the heart of his criminal empire, right to the inn where not even his assassins were allowed to visit.

True, not too long ago, Bronwyn brought in Wilder, but the difference was that Wilder he liked.

Out of all the men his darling girl could bring home, why would she bring in a necromancy hating, ghost hunting *priest* of all things?

If Elwis was a religious man, he would pray for patience, but since he wasn't anything of the sort he simply watched.

And waited.

And plotted.

He didn't know what this *Evengi Ichabod* was up to, but he doubted his motives were pure. Elwis saw the way he looked at his daughter, as if she was some princess in need of saving and he was her gallant knight who would sweep in and rescue her. But rescue her from what?

Why Elwis presumed from himself.

Elwis leaned over the railing watching Evengi put a log into the fire as he told Natasya a story. Whatever it was, it must be terribly amusing because her laughter rang up to where he was sitting. Whatever course of action he took, he would have to proceed carefully.

Because as much as he distrusted this Evengi he had never seen his daughter smile so wide. She has changed since he sent her to Sunder Hollow. She carried a weight of sadness now, but also a vibrant happiness.

And Evengi was responsible for the happiness at least. Elwis never wanted to be accused of taking his daughter's happiness from her. His girls were more important to him than the whole of Ruskhazar.

So, for now, he would simply have to tolerate this Evengi. Sleep with one eye open and wait to see what Evengi was up to. He would hope that Natasya would realize that she and the priest were simply not compatible.

Or...

Elwis smirked as he played a second option through his mind. Because while Evengi Ichabod may be nothing more than a pest to him, he could find a use for Ivan Fyodorov.

He had heard rumors that the Fyodorov girl had somehow survived the assassination attempt. Rumors that she was traveling with a guardsman under a special assignment from none other than the Eyes and the Ears of the King.

Oh, but that wasn't even the best part. Because the rumors also claimed that the guardsman was none other than the illegitimate son of the king. And if some tragedies were to befall the rest of the family... why this boy would be the rightful heir to the throne.

But of course... those were just rumors and speculation. There was no point in bringing them up for now. Not until he had succeeded in killing the current king.

Then it was up to the Eyes and the Ears of the King to put the guardsman on the throne. It was up to Alya Fyodorov to marry the guardsman.

And it was up to his sweet little Natasya to keep the man who will one day be the brother-in-law to the king caught in his snare.

MORE STORIES FROM RUSKHAZAR

Don't Miss These Other Books Set in Ruskhazar

Read Bronwyn's story in...

Trapped by Magic

Read Alya's story in...

The Gods Created Monsters (*What the Gods Did*, book one)

The Gods Lost Their Way (*What the Gods Did*, book two)

Get more about Elwis the Eel in...

Between Gods and Demigods (*Rage Like the Gods,* book 0.5)

Rage Like the Gods (*Rage Like the Gods,* book one)

Check out another Ruskhazar Standalone:

A Tale of Gods and Glory

ABOUT THE AUTHOR

Nicki is a twenty-something author of fantasy and YA. She has been writing since she was eleven, and has since published several works. She enjoys creating stories with twisty-stabby faerie romances, retellings that take a darker turn, and epic fantasies in worlds full of monsters and magic. Nicki lives in Ohio where she spends far too much time watching TV, playing video games, and sleeping. She listens to music basically all the time, and adores obsessing over mythologies, her shows, and her slew of fictional boyfriends. When not writing, she can usually be found at her desk with either a paintbrush or a pen in her hand.

Acknowledgements

Every book is special because it's a product of my imagination and was born through my passion. But this story is special because I got to share a part of that creative process with other fellow authors.

So, this is a thank you to the authors who chose to be a part of my vision. You guys were the best through thick and thin and sudden change in plans so here's a special thanks to Jes, Celeste, and Cait. This was my first time creating a series like this so thank you for taking a chance on my brainchild.

To my family for being my support system. Caleb, did you notice that mention of Creed?

To my readers for being a part of this author's journey with me. You guys are what makes writing worth it, knowing that I actually get to share these stories with an amazing audience.

To my dragons for being the most amazing street team ever.

To my editor Eve for the wonderful work that you did.

To my cover designers Maria and Amira for everything that you did to bring my ideas to life. And to Maddy for the gorgeous character illustrations of Natasya and Evengi. And to Chaim for the gorgeous map.

To Jesus for coming back from the dead.

MORE TITLES BY NICKI CHAPELWAY

Of Gold and Iron (*The Of Dreams and Nightmares trilogy,* book one)
Of Stars and Shadows (*The Of Dreams and Nightmares trilogy,* book two)
Of Dawn and Fire (*The Of Dreams and Nightmares trilogy,* book three)

Bound by Knighthood

An Apprentice of Death (*An Apprentice of Death,* book one)
A House of Blood (*And Apprentice of Death,* book two)

A Winter Grim and Lonely (*Winter Cursed,* book 0.5)
Winter Cursed (*Winter Cursed,* book one)
A Winter Dark and Deadly (*Winter Cursed,* book two)

Harbinger of the End: A Tale of Loki and Sigyn

NICKI CHAPELWAY

And They All Bow Down

SEASONS OF LEGEND

This Hollow Heart is the first book in the Seasons of Legend series, a multi-author collection of no-spice romantic fantasy novellas designed to be read independently. Each standalone features a different season and retelling with an enemies to lover's twist. Here is the rest of the series:

Autumn — This Hollow Heart by Nicki Chapelway — A Sleepy Hollow Retelling — October 1, 2024

Winter — This Frozen Heart by Jes Drew — A Snow Queen Retelling — December 1, 2024

Spring — This Rotting Heart by Celeste Baxendell — A Hades & Persephone Retelling — April 1, 2025

Summer — This Midsummer Heart by C.K. Beggan — A Midsummer Night's Dream Retelling — June 1, 2025

Made in the USA
Las Vegas, NV
19 October 2024